SEA-WOLF HUNTER

By the same author

Ben Grant Stories

A Capful of Glory
Gruesome Tide
The Monday Mutiny
Secret of the Kara Sea
The Gemini Plot
Ninety Feet to the Sun
     *
Atlantic Encounter
Eye of the Eagle

Sea-Wolf Hunter

A Ben Grant Story

Eric J. Collenette

KIMBER FICTION

© Eric J. Collenette, 1989

All rights reserved. No part of this publication may be reproduced, stored in a retrieval system or transmitted, in any form or by any means, electronic, mechanical, photocopying, recording or otherwise, without prior permission in writing from William Kimber & Co Ltd.

First published in 1989

British Library Cataloguing in Publication Data

Collenette, Eric J.
Sea-wolf hunter
I. Title
823'.914 [F]

ISBN 0-7183-0725-9

William Kimber & Co Ltd is part of the Thorsons Publishing Group, Wellingborough, Northamptonshire, NN8 2RQ, England.

Printed in Great Britain by
Billing & Sons Limited, Worcester

1 3 5 7 9 10 8 6 4 2

To pluck bright honour from the pale-faced moon,
  Or dive into the bottom of the deep.
Where fathom-line could never touch the ground,
  And pluck up drowned honour by the locks.

William Shakespeare 1564–1616

One

The long corridor is a resonant, echoing chamber as our heels click smartly on the tiled floor. We are heading for a long-awaited interview with a group of very senior officers, and my companion is an old shipmate from the days of Dunkirk, Lieutenant-Commander Martingale. He has overcome a lot of prejudice and animosity to become a submarine commander, and would have progressed much faster if only he had learned to toe the line and refrained from bucking the system whenever he felt frustrated by red tape, but it says a lot for his personality and reputation as a submarine officer that he has achieved this much. There are certain senior officers who regard him as a threat to their authority, and a bad influence on others who might consider throwing aside the manual and exercising their brains.

He has the looks to match his personality: slightly pugnacious, with a stubborn set to his jaw, and dark intelligent eyes. He has never taken kindly to service protocol, and he is far too outspoken for one who seeks promotion. Once he develops an idea in his head nothing deters him, which is why I find myself striding alongside him now, as we prepare to place his proposals before a detracting bunch of cynics.

It is autumn 1941, just weeks after the capture of *U–570*, which surrendered to a Coastal Command Hudson and allowed herself to be towed into Iceland and beached. When the experts have done with her she will be renamed HMS *Graph*, and there are many high-ranking people who would like to get their hands on her for all sorts of reasons. So it is not surprising that Martingale finds himself at the bottom of the pile when he has the cheek to ask for her.

He is convinced that he has a use for her that supersedes

anything else; although he knows as well as I do that he stands small chance of getting what he wants. In fact, he would not have got this far if it was not for an influential ally in the shape of Rear Admiral Emery Fox, who knows a good man when he sees one and sees in Martingale a reincarnation of himself as a young, junior officer struggling to overcome prejudice and bigotry. Without his help we would not have got an initial hearing, let alone an audience with this lot.

We reach a small ante-room with a glass-domed roof that permits the November sunshine to bleach the white walls and plush furnishings. Angled across one corner is a large mahogany desk with a nice-looking Wren sitting behind it. She looks up at us with friendly eyes, and I am pleasantly surprised to note that I get equal shares of her greeting before she focuses on him.

'Lieutenant-Commander Martingale?'

His dark eyes light up as he returns her smile, and I find myself fading into the background. 'That's right,' he simpers. 'I have an appointment with the admiral.'

She rises to come round the desk. 'He is not quite ready for you, but I'll let him know that you are here if you will take a seat for a moment.' She raps softly on an oak-panelled door and slides through, leaving us standing in the hushed sanctity of this inner chamber. I glance towards the chairs lining the wall, but take my cue from him and remain standing. This is foreign territory for one of such lowly rank and I need all the stature I can get.

I am beginning to sweat before the door sighs open again to admit a dapper flag lieutenant. He wears a set smile on his pale face, and pointedly stares right through me. 'I know who you are, sir, but who is your companion?'

Martingale nods towards me. 'You'll find he can talk, lieutenant. Why don't you ask him?'

'Chief Petty Officer Grant, sir,' I state firmly.

He doesn't take his eyes from Martingale. 'Is he with you, sir?'

'Yes.'

The eyes shift a little and he runs a finger inside his tight collar. 'We were not expecting anyone but you,' he complains petulantly.

'Were you not?'

The flag officer fidgets uncomfortably and coughs when he sees he is not going to get any more of an explanation. 'Will you come this way please? The admiral is extremely busy, so I hope you will make your request as succinctly as possible.'

'Don't concern yourself, lieutenant. I am as eager as you to get this over with.'

The Wren is holding the door wide open as we go through. She smells fresh and expensive, and her hair shines liquid black in the blatant sunlight.

The inner office is heavy with cigar smoke and rich with the smell of good leather. Stretched right down the centre is a long table, large enough to use as a bowling alley, with blotting pads set out at precise intervals, and cut-glass tumblers glinting like a row of incandescent guardsmen. Even the particles of dust dancing in the shafting light from the tall windows have an expensive look about them. The rear admiral and three four-ringed captains sit staring up as the flag lieutenant introduces us.

We stand rigidly at attention under their concerted gaze until the admiral waves a generous hand towards the chairs on his left. It leaves us facing the three captains while he presides from the head of the table. 'Please carry on,' he booms, in a voice used to yelling against Atlantic gales.

Martingale has rehearsed his spiel for some time and launches into a long monologue. If enthusiasm and attention to precise detail were all that was required he would win hands down. They study his face and allow him to continue uninterrupted until he is finished. It is a straightforward plan, and he receives a nod of approval from time to time from the admiral. However, the captains keep their faces wooden as he explains how Dönitz's U-boats are at their most vulnerable after they have made their attack on a convoy at night and run out astern to reload their tubes. They are silhouetted by the glow of 'snowflake' rockets from the convoy, and often the glare from a burning tanker. In rough weather they must dive to provide a steady working platform for their torpedomen, creeping along at slow speed while they rearm themselves. That is when Martingale would like to be waiting with a submarine – preferably *U–570*.

Up to that last suggestion they are listening with grudging approval, and I can see the fighting spirit in their eyes as he sets the scene; but the moment he mentions the U–boat their eyes change. They have no intention of offering such a valuable prize to a mere lieutenant-commander.

'I am curious to learn how you became involved with the interrogation of the prisoners,' declares one of the captains with large tufts of grey hair sprouting from prominent cheekbones to give him a satanic look. 'I thought that our intelligence people had that in hand.'

'It was my idea,' declares the admiral quickly. 'It takes an age for the experts' reports to filter back to us, and I thought that it would do no harm to learn what basic differences, if any, exist between their submariners and ours. Know your enemy, gentlemen. Find out what makes him tick. I'm sure you will agree that it is a useful exercise. He will have some idea of the type of man he is up against when he takes command of *Tarantula*.'

'What did you find out that our intelligence people have not already discovered?' sneers an ample-bellied captain with about six chins. 'Surely they have the experience. I am amazed that they did not resent your interference.'

The admiral sighs deeply. 'It was on an entirely different level: more like a series of informal chats. That is why he took Chief Petty Officer Grant along with him. We believed that NCOs would talk more readily to other NCOs. It was an experiment on my part, and it remains to be seen whether it was of any value. Perhaps you will explain what you did learn, Martingale.'

'I was looking for attitude rather than hard facts, sir. The enemy is turning out U–boats at a fast rate and I reckoned that they must be finding it difficult to man them with quality crews.' He looks at their faces. 'After all, it is a pretty lousy job, and there must be a limit even in Nazi Germany to suicidal maniacs. Even when things are going well for them, and they are sinking ships right left and centre, they face long weeks of strain in appalling living conditions, and that requires a special sort of man, as we well know. Their boats are smaller than ours, and their living conditions even more spartan. They do much longer patrols than us, generally speaking. I wanted to find out if there is a weakness somewhere in their make-up now that many of their most experienced men have gone.'

'The official report says that *U-570*'s company was a mixture of hard-lined Nazis and non-Hitlerites,' says the captain with the hairy cheeks.

'They are *all* Nazis as far as I am concerned, sir,' says Martingale in a harsh voice. 'They wear the uniform, and they pull the trigger. I cannot accept that there is more than one type of enemy. They will be proud enough to be part of the master race if they win the bloody war.'

The admiral turns to me. 'What about the rankers, chief? What is your opinion of them?'

I clear my throat. I have never held the attention of so much top brass. 'The young ones are dedicated Nazis, sir. All convinced that they are going to rule the world. The older hands are less convinced. They tell me that *U-570* has only been at sea a few days and that the skipper has never done a full operational war patrol. Many of them were seasick, most were fed up to the teeth, and it sounds as though there was a lot of arguing, even fighting amongst the crew. One of the senior hands told me that he had never sailed with such a lot of useless no-hopers.'

The captain. 'The report also says that the first watch officer is a Nazi, but the second is not. Is that so?'

'As I said before, sir, some are more fanatical than others. The only man I could find with a completely open mind was the engineer. I don't think he'd care whose side he was on as long as he was allowed to run his diesels.' He hesitates for a moment, looking into each of their faces. 'There is no doubt that Germany is building submarines faster than they can find quality crews to man them. In their service the captain *is* the boat: even more than in ours. His personality and commitment holds the crew together, and if he is even slightly under par it reflects on their performance. Kapitänleutnant Rahmlow was unblooded and untried when compared to some of his more aggressive colleagues. The Priens and the Kretschmers have gone now, and the new breed consists of men with high ideals but small experience. What Grant says is true, sir. *U-570* is a brand new boat, and had been at sea only four days before she was forced to dive in a hurry to avoid a Sunderland flying boat, where she hit a submerged reef. They carried out some hasty repairs at Trondheim, but she still went back to sea with a faulty sound detector, other minor problems, and a very inexperienced commander. It is no wonder that they did not show up well when the stakes were down.' He leans forward to emphasize his point. 'I believe there are more like him, and it gives us an edge over them: I'd like to prove it.'

'Submarines against submarines is no few formula,' declares the tubby captain disdainfully. 'The "R" boats were designed for that very purpose back in the 1919s. We require boats urgently in the Mediterranean to stop supplies getting through to the Afrika Korps. We cannot spare our own submarines for such an unproven exercise. Let alone *U–570*. In my opinion your proposal is a dead duck.'

One captain has sat through it all without making a comment. He is a lean man with a hungry look and haunting eyes. Now he leans forward to declare forcefully, 'I have to differ with you there, Boxwell. We could do with an injection of something new into the Atlantic to boost morale. Our escorts are stretched to the limit, their leaders torn between allowing ships to go chasing after shadows and weakening the screen, or maintaining close defence. Until we can organise full support groups to take some of the weight off the close escorts the U–boats have it much their own way. I would love to see a few of Dönitz's heroes get the shock of their lives when they find themselves at the business end of someone else's torpedoes for a change.' He looks away into the distance for a moment as though he is looking at an imprinted memory of something terrible. 'They seldom attack in daylight if they have the choice, sir,' he tells the admiral. 'The last thing they would expect is to find an alien submarine in their midst during a consorted attack. Before they rumble the truth I believe that Martingale has every chance of wreaking havoc amongst them.'

'However,' he turns back towards us, 'in the darkness one boat is much like another, and your "T" class packs a bigger punch than the standard U–boat. Therefore, my recommendation is that we allow you the opportunity to prove your point with *Tarantula*. Remember one thing, though. Don't expect any mercy from the escorts. They won't have the time or the inclination to ask questions if they see or hear a submarine, and

I won't cramp their style by warning them. There is no way we can guarantee you immunity from our own depth-charges.'

There is a moment's silence while the admiral allows them to absorb it all, then he asks, 'Are there any objections?'

'I remain unconvinced, but I imagine that I am in the minority,' pouts the tubby captain. 'I have never liked mavericks, and when I look at your record I see that is exactly what you are, Martingale. However, at least we are not going to turn you loose with our new acquisition.' He chortles as he goes on sardonically, 'Why don't you find a U–boat of your own to play with?'

After that we are dismissed and walk out into the sunshine with a feeling of quiet satisfaction. I stride in step for a while as he broods over the outcome. I reckon that we have got as much as we could have dared hope for, and it would have been a bloody miracle if they had granted him the U–boat, but it is hard to tell what is going through his mind as we merge with the dockyard traffic. Suddenly he stops dead, and two dockyard mateys almost run into our sterns. 'That would really be something, wouldn't it?'

I stare at him. 'What would, sir?'

'To capture another U–boat. One is a hell of an achievement, but another would really be a slap in the face for Dönitz.'

He turns to stride on, leaving me to hurry after him. We bustle through the crowd of brown-overalled workers and naval personnel, alongside the tall, featureless dockyard wall until we emerge through the gate into the road. He could have insisted on a boat to take him back to the base, but he prefers to walk with me. There is a trickle of commuters scurrying busily past the harbour station towards the Gosport Ferry, and we join them as the skipper holds her against the pull of a short mooring-rope with a slow-turning screw while his passengers board.

The harbour stretches like an old, threadbare carpet towards Porchester Creek. A sort of dead olive-green, with a sprinkling of small craft weaving between the sleeping grey warships. Passengers cram into corners and prepare to while away the short journey, wrapped in their own problems. They are used to war now, and some find it hard to remember a time when there were no white-painted kerbs or taped windows. The wail of a siren no longer has the sharp, knife-edged thrill of alarm, and they can absorb the abominable noises of the night with apathetic disdain. Their biggest concern is knowing when a consignment of fresh eggs comes into a local shop and how to obtain a good place in the queue that forms like magic when the rumour spreads. They look shabby in their over-worn garments, made to outlive their natural life with diligent needlework.

The kids old enough to remember dream of real bananas and counters laden with sweets and chocolate. They carry their gasmasks and learn how to file down into the shelter when the sirens sound. Even the stray mongrels that roam the streets know enough to take cover when they see the barrage balloons ascend. War has become a continuing drudgery, and in this great naval port they know more than most how much their future depends on convoys of dark ships getting through.

When I look out of the window I see the other ferry passing down the port side with a matching cargo of humanity. Soon we are nosing into the opposite pier and a new flood of people spills out across the causeway. We join it as it spreads in all directions, past the bus terminus and into the town.

In true Martingale fashion he sets aside protocol that says officers should not hob-nob with ratings on shore, and insists on walking back to blockhouse with me, so that he can expound on the plans he has in mind for *Tarantula*. We take the footpath that runs along the edge of Haslar Creek, on the opposite shore to the submarine base. It is within stone-throwing distance, but we have to go the long way round the estuary in order to reach it, and that allows plenty of time for him to get his thoughts in order.

The short November day is drawing to a close and the colours fading into sombre greys and blacks, while the sullen, murky water laps disconsolately amongst garbage and sad-looking reeds lining the bank. Buildings muffle traffic noise, so that we are left with the softer sounds of the creek as it beds down for the night. Above our heads ponderous clouds roll in from the west, driven by a growing wind that holds the promise of a gale on its breath. I'll be glad to get back on the main road before it gets dark, for the blackout makes this path dangerous with its potholes and sharp corners.

'We have a lot of hard work ahead of us, Grant.'
'Yes, sir.'

I wait patiently for him to assemble his thoughts. There is a bite in the air now, and our breath hangs visible as we trudge along in step.

'I want every man to feel important: that he has a vital part to play, and is not just a cog in the machinery. I want to know about any bad apples, so that we can root them out, put them in positions where they can be watched, or get rid of them. There will be no second chances. The first lieutenant knows my views on this, but you are closer to the troops than we are, so it is up to you to get together with the other chiefs and POs to find out if there are any special talents amongst them, regardless of their ratings. We will be concentrating on night exercises, and this will be a more intense working-up than you have ever known. I intend to introduce a whole new system of night action stations, apart from the normal diving station they have become used to.'

I listen quietly. There is nothing new in having men jump from one job to another in boats; it is something we encourage, but he is talking about something more than that.

'If a stoker has better night vision than an AB we'll swop them over. We'll teach the AB to man a ballast pump or whatever, while the stoker stands watch on the bridge with a pair of binoculars. I want people who can see in the dark and recognise shadows for what they are. To read the night like a book in all kinds of weather. It never ceases to amaze me that we train a man to make reports in the correct, service manner, and then leave him to get on with it.'

He strides on for a moment, musing over his ideas. 'I am going to plague the life out of our masters to allow us plenty of practice at night-encounter exercises with the training boat. It won't do much for the crew's social life, and they will probably be happy to see the back of us, but there are no short cuts if we are to succeed.'

'Yes, sir.' I guide him past a post that encroaches onto the path. He is totally absorbed as we stumble along. Suddenly he swings on me. 'How do you think our lads will react?'

My immediate reaction is to say, 'They'll do as they are bloody-well told,' because I don't believe that there is room in this war for concern over the feelings of subordinates. However, I tone my response down a little. 'So long as they know why they are being driven they'll put their backs into it, sir. It's when they are treated like mindless morons that they begin to rebel.'

'That's my thought exactly. There will be no more twenty-one day patrols as far as we are concerned. If I have my way we will refuel from ships in convoy and draw our torpedoes and supplies from the escorts at sea so that we can remain on station for long periods. We will be on call whenever a wolf pack is forming up to attack, and we can't do that if we are scurrying off to base every three weeks from the middle of the Atlantic.'

We are out on the road now, with the white kerb to guide us through the solid darkness. My thoughts go to even darker nights at sea when the wind is full of spray and the boat is jumping about like a mad thing. There will be shadows everywhere on such nights, real and imagined. We will be on our own, for no friendly ship is going to risk a torpedo in the guts while they try to identify a submarine. Faces will be raw and eyes red-rimmed with fatigue as we stare out into the night for one of Dönitz's boats to appear low down in the water. At first they won't know what hit them, but they will get wise to us after a while, and then it will be boat against boat, and keen-eyed lookouts will be at a premium. When I think about it I can appreciate his concern for the state of mind of our men.

At the gate we split up to go our own ways, he to the wardroom, while I stride along to the chiefs' mess for a hot shower and a bite to eat. In the morning I am due to travel up north to Birkenhead, where Cammell Laird's blokes are putting the final touches to *Tarantula* after her acceptance trials. For the first time she will have a full naval crew. The commissioning ceremony will take place three days from now.

I feel the need to get away from Dolphin for a while and put my mind on other things. So, when one of the chiefs suggests a trip across to watch an ENSA show in Portsmouth Barracks I am more than glad to accept his offer.

As so often happens, when you do something on the spur of the moment it turns out to be a success. Mainly because of a pianist who tops the bill and plays popular classics to the enthralled audience. The motley crowd of ribald sailors who responded raucously to the previous assortment of comedians, dancers, paper tearers and crooners settle into their seats, tamed and quiet as they listen spellbound to her fingers pouring out Chopin and others. I have never known a bunch of matelots yet who cannot be seduced by a good pianist.

This lady is full of talent, and she knows just what to play. The half-familiar themes that most of her audience have whistled and hummed in their messdecks, on the guns, or in tune with the turbines fills the hall and reaches down right into their souls. At the end they refuse to let her go. In the midst of all the drabness of broken buildings and wartime squalor her music is a tonic, and for a while they forget grey ships, grey seas, and the oil-soaked men they pick up from broken ships in that other world.

Finally we have to let her go, and I wait with my companion for the crush to ease before following the crowd towards the exit. It has been a perfect evening, and we got through it without interruption from the Luftwaffe.

'Chief Petty Officer Grant!'

I recognise the voice at once, and swing round to find her pushing through a small knot of her mates towards me. She shouldn't smile at blokes like that; it's enough to turn them to jelly. 'I'm glad that I've caught you,' she pants. 'There is something I think you should know before you travel north.'

My mate nods to say that he'll wait outside, and I edge her away from the crowd. I'm no expert on beauty but she'll do for me with her stylish features and honest eyes. She has the sort of smile that warms my inside, and it comes from deep down; you can see that just by looking at her. With her page-boy hair-do and her neat figure tucked into the Wren's uniform she looks good enough to eat.

'Captain Boxwell is to be your boss at Rothesay. He will be responsible for the whole training schedule.'

Something in her tone makes me suspicious. 'Which one was Captain Boxwell?'

'I am afraid it was the one with all the chins and the pregnant belly.'

I grin at her description. 'He doesn't sound like your favourite person.'

'He is no one's favourite person – except maybe his own, and I'm sad to say, he is my boss.'

'I got the impression that he was not over-enthralled with the skipper's ideas.'

She nods soberly. 'Not only that; he has little time for Lieutenant-Commander Martingale either. Captain Boxwell has his own ideas on social status and service protocol. As far as he is concerned anyone below the rank of full captain should be seen and not heard, and not step out of line like your worthy captain is inclined to do. He also hates being contradicted, and he can come up with a thousand good reasons why *Tarantula* should not be spared for what he considers a madcap scheme. I believe he will try everything to prove his point and put a stop to your project.'

'There are plenty like him about,' I grunt. 'But it seems a bit daft putting someone in charge of something when he has no faith in it. We'll need all the support we can get if Martingale is to stand a chance of getting it off the ground.'

'You must understand that whatever else he may be, Boxwell is considered to be an expert on anti-submarine warfare. He lectures on the subject at naval establishments throughout the world, and has a specialist knowledge of detection apparatus. That is why he holds the rank of captain. He is a hard man to convince at the best of times, but if he is biased against you he can make life extremely difficult.'

I look down into her serious eyes for a moment, then break into a smile. 'You have stuck your neck out to tell me this, haven't you?'

She gets a little indignant. 'I've told you nothing that you could not find out officially within the next few days. Forewarned is fore–armed, and I don't believe one side should hold all the aces.'

'Don't worry too much about Martingale. He has stood up to many Boxwells in his time.'

She smiles and the tension eases, 'And what about you? Are you not just as stubborn as he?'

We are moving towards the door now, past cleaners who are bustling about tidying up. There are a few envious glances from some of them. 'We are two of a kind, I suppose,' I say quietly. 'The big difference is that he has a hell of a lot more to lose than I have.'

She grins. 'You forget I learn many things in my job. You both create waves from time to time, and I know about your time in Norway. You have made quite a name for yourself, Chief Petty Officer Grant.'

She is teasing me now, and I'm wallowing in it. I am thinking what a lucky bastard Martingale is and wondering if he appreciates it. Just looking at her makes me feel good. My voice is a little trite when I say, 'I'll pass on your message, I'm sure he will be most grateful.'

Her expression alters slightly. 'I hope that you will be a little grateful yourself.'

'Of course,' I say quickly, feeling a bit queer as she looks up at me with those big brown eyes.

'I'm glad,' she says. 'You see, I am being sent to Scotland as well, as Captain Boxwell's secretary. So there is every chance of seeing each other during the next few weeks.'

'You and Martingale?'

'No, you fool; you and I.'

I stare after her as she trots off to join her mates. I have some strange thoughts running through my head as the other chief makes impatient noises at my side. Captain's secretaries do not usually consort with us peasants from the lower deck, yet I would have to be blind or daft not to realise that she is being more than a little friendly.

'Heh!' I exclaim, jerking us both to a halt. 'I don't even know her bloody name!'

Two

The boat judders and heaves her shoulders over an incoming swell, throwing half a ton of solid green water over the bridge and its occupants when it plunges its bow deep into the next roller. She seems to be enjoying her first experience of a force eighter, while we on the bridge duck and cringe as we are deluged. Apart from receiving collarfuls of ice cold spray it is an exhilarating pastime as Martingale drives her northwards, making no concession to the weather.

We are wrapped up like eskimos in oilskins and dufflecoats as we peer out at the shadowy squalls that sweep in from the west. Beyond the veils of driving rain the bleak ramparts of Scotland's cliffs lift into the overcast sky as we bring Corsewall Light abreast on our starboard beam and search the haze on our port bow for a glimpse of Ailsa Craig. It is a mucky day, with seagulls riding the blustering wind above us, and lowering clouds spreading gloom across an olive sea. There is a strange beauty too as the whitecaps surge by, and the waves unfold to bear down on us. The boat is very small in such a wilderness of broken water that seems determined to cut us down to size when we peer out from our low platform at the high ridges cutting into the sky.

Quite a number of the crew are seasick, for it is a new kind of motion to new submariners, nothing like the kind they have become used to in other ships. I know some of the older hands, for the submarine service is a close-knit community. There is 'Jumbo' Moore for instance: the big, six-foot-three second coxswain with shoulders like a barn door, who has learned the art of manipulating his hefty shape through a boat with remarkable ease. He runs the casing with a rod of iron, yet no one can recall him ever resorting to violence, although it must be said that few have been foolish enough to give him cause. When he squats on the seat beside me at diving stations, manning the forward hydroplanes, he crouches over the dials and wheel like a big, black bear, dominating the control room.

One of the most important blokes in the boat is Petty Officer Trump, our HSD (Higher Submarine Detector). When he has not got his head stuck in a book he sits inside his small asdic cabinet with his earphones clamped on his head, deciphering a weird symphony of under-water noises that would baffle ordinary people. He translates the rebounding pings from the super-sonic pulses sent out by his oscillator, sorting out the solid, metallic contacts from fish and other undersea disturbances. Apart from his ears he must use his imagination to interpret the strange pattern of lines on the rotating iodised roll of paper that turns the pulses into visual images, and paints a picture of the seabed when we nose into the shallows. On a good day, when the sea is calm and there are not changes of temperature to create dense patches of ocean to confuse the set, or interference from screws of other ships to blot out true echoes, a good operator can distinguish the hard contact of a submarine from other spurious sounds with quiet efficiency. Such men are invaluable, and it is unfortunate that in prewar days when gunnery was all the rage, small importance was given to this strange breed. Even now many of the old guard refuse to take them seriously, and consider the 'ping bos'ns' to be slightly crazy. After all, who could listen to those incessant, water-torture pings for long without going barmy? We have yet to find out just how good he is, but he comes with a fine pedigree.

It will take time to work out who belongs where. There will be some who come along just for the ride, and do as little as possible to earn their bread, and the odd man who cannot be left unsupervised, and we have to slot them into jobs that require the minimum of brain-power and imagination. They will still provide a useful service by allowing the more competent to carry out more demanding duties. No one's absolutely useless, for they have all served in general service ships, and been through the initial period of special training and examination required by those who come into submarines, and for the very few who slip through the net and never amount to much, there are the vast majority to keep them in order.

In such a small, closely knit service the men with time under their belts bring their own reputations with them from other boats. It is a case of fitting everyone into his slot, and getting the whole company working as a team in the shortest time possible, so that *Tarantula* is made into an efficient fighting unit before we go out looking for trouble with the Germans.

The man mainly responsible for making those decisions is on the bridge now, taking bearings from landmarks sliding past our starboard side, to obtain a running fix. Our first lieutenant is a flamboyant, slightly eccentric character whose real name is Morley, but who is known throughout the submarine service as 'Falstaff', because of his rotund, gnome-like appearance and his obsession with Shakespeare. He has never been known to miss an opportunity to quote the bard.

Martingale could not have found a better second-in-command, for he is a reliable, popular officer who should have had his own command, if it was not for an unfortunate reputation for being something of a wild man when he has a few drinks inside him. The fact that he never drinks at sea doesn't seem to impress those who make the decisions, and he must wait until his new captain's reports sweep aside prejudice. His reputation stems from the days when he used his stocky, tank-like body as a battering-ram on the rugby field, and he still sees no reason why he should side-step when he can bulldoze his way through a problem.

Now he is passing bearings down through the voicepipe to the helmsman so they can be relayed to the navigator and plotted onto the chart. A long-winded process, but it is too wet and windy up here in this small cockpit to manipulate dividers and parallel rulers, and at such times, when they are 'shooting' the sun or the stars, I am brought up from below to provide an extra pair of eyes.

Today we are running in towards the Firth of Clyde with the loom of the Scottish coast closing in from starboard. The lookouts must not be allowed to become lulled into a false sense of security even though we can see the occasional house on the cliffs, for there is every chance of a stray enemy bomber gliding in through a gap in the grey overcast with its engines throttled back so that we will not hear it until it is on top of us. The grey shape would be hard to see against the lowering sky, and there would be little enough time to decide whether to fight it out on the surface or pull the plug and get below. With the best-drilled crew it takes half a minute to dive, and even longer to swim away from the swirl of disturbed water before the bombs come whistling down.

I glance at them, and find them diligently concentrating on their sectors. They have an additional problem today as they try to keep their lenses dry with periscope paper. We can see the occasional vehicle on the mainland as we glide past Ailsa Craig, heading for the channel between Great Cumbrae Island and Brushag Point, then on round the corner towards the Kyles of Bute and Rothesay Bay. There is romance in those names. Already I fancy I can taste the tang of heather and gorse as I breathe the keen air. Despite the greyness of the day there is a wild beauty in the surrounding hills and buffetting greybacks that mottle the surface on every side.

'So foul and fair a day I have not seen.' Falstaff has completed his observations. 'Blow, blow, thou winter wind – thou art not so unkind as man's ingratitude.'

'Yes, sir,' I respond obliquely. 'You can almost hear the haggis playing in the heather.'

'You are a savage, Grant, like the rest of your philistine friends. To us golfers this is Mecca. Nowhere in the world does a small white orb sing more sweetly through the air.'

'If you are done with me I will retire below to my paperwork, sir. You will want me to have my requisitions ready as soon as we are alongside the depot ship.'

'Aye, do that, and call our noble captain. Convey my compliments and tell him the Craig is coming abreast and the air bites shrewdly on the bridge.'

I leave him ducking the spray as I go blustering down through the tower with the downdraught tugging at my oilskins until I drop into the control room.

The gunlayer is on the helm, and the control room log-keeper squatting behind him. There could be no more contrasting men than these two. The craggy-faced gunlayer with his broken nose and pugnacious features who dreams about the time when he will once more sit behind the steering wheel of his double-decker bus in the London traffic, and the skinny torpedoman with the big, soulful eyes and oversized feet. His name is Perry, but everyone calls him 'Clump' because of his size ten boots.

I have to squeeze past the navigator's bony rump as he bends over his chart-table. He is a studious man who needs a reminder now and again that the navy demands a certain amount of discipline, and he should play his part, even though it goes against the grain. He and the engineer would like to ignore all military aspects of their duties to concentrate on their special skills. Apart from navigating he is our Asdic officer, and he and Petty Officer Trump make a good pair as they sort out the weird sounds that emanate from the box of tricks in their small office. The snag is that they tend to ignore everyone else in the process.

I am just in time for a mug of thick soup as I slide into the muggy warmth of the chiefs' mess. With still a couple of hours to go before we have to prepare for berthing I decide to ask permission to issue the rum when I have finished my soup. The diesels rumble their comfortable melody and conversation is muted, so I spend a few moments with my rum and my thoughts.

Martingale was non-committal when I told him about Boxwell's appointment, but I see his mouth tighten and know that he is not too pleased. We will need all the support we can get during the training programme. Already the navigator has been trying to arrange for our Asdic operators to go to the training teacher at Londonderry, where they have a mock-up of a destroyer's Asdic cabinet that can simulate real conditions, right down to the pitch and roll of a ship at sea. Trump and his team require all the practical experience they can get if they are to distinguish the different sounds they will hear when we are out there on the fringes of a convoy at night. We will rely on them more than ever this trip, when we are scratching around blindly for the first contact of an enemy U–boat, and even when we succeed in locating one it will be up to them to keep us one jump ahead of the other boat.

Already we are swopping men about as we try out their strengths and weaknesses. Soon we must decide on the full team and begin to run through the various drills over and over until they can react almost without thinking, and cope with all sorts of unexpected urgencies automatically.

It requires a certain amount of diplomacy and tact to overcome inter-branch jealousy and pride as we shift them about regardless of the badges they wear on their sleeves. Teamwork takes on a new meaning under Martingale's command. He is turning the whole boat into a single attack unit, with each man fully dependent on his neighbour when the boat goes into her anti-submarine routine. The intelligent ones amongst them know what they are good at, and relish the opportunity to exercise their skills, though there are the inevitable few who sulk at the way he manipulates them, but they are in the minority, and we ignore all their protestations.

The skipper spares no one as he tries out his new ideas. We hold meetings in the wardroom far into the night, and he asks senior hands for their suggestions and theories on how to improve the attack procedures. The whole crew becomes involved, and is encouraged to voice ideas on how to make their tasks easier and more effective. The local training boat's captain learns to change direction quickly when he sees Martingale approaching along the deck of the depot ship, for he knows he will be pestered for yet another night-encounter exercise, or some new unorthodox tactic that goes far beyond the normal working-up drill he has carried out with other boats. His men curse their lack of shore-leave as our skipper refuses to pack up at the end of a long day, and insists on yet another exercise to practise night-encounters over and over in order to improve the ability of our lookouts to recognise targets at night, in the open sea. Many times we return to the depot ship when it is too late to even think about getting cleaned into shore-going rig in time to catch the last liberty boat.

To all intent the other boat becomes an enemy U–boat, using every trick in the book to evade us and work herself into a position to retaliate with a broadside of her own. Soon they catch the spirit of the game and her skipper proves to be no slouch as he piles on the pressure with so much enthusiasm that it almost ends with a collision.

We have come well past the initial stages of carrying out mock attacks while the H–boat tows 'buffs' on the surface to mark her position, enabling our Asdic team to gain experience of the sound of a boat creeping along on a steady course. They have learned to distinguish the 'doppler' effect so they know if a boat is moving away, turning toward, or running beam-on to us. They recognise the noise of her blowing tanks or flooding up, increasing speed or lying dormant. We graduate from the calm waters of the lochs where there was little disturbance to produce 'quenching' to confuse the echoes and hydrophone responses. Ears are becoming tuned to the sharp, metallic ping of a definite contact as opposed to that of a shoal of fish or a patch of high-density water which can return freak echoes. A good operator must exercise his imagination as well as his skill to gain a good contact and hold it. That is when the true experts emerge, and we soon realise that there is none better than Trump as we leave behind the sheltered water and the buffs to run out into the open sea for more intensive drill. We work in all kinds of weather and conditions until Trump's men know the sound of all kinds of propellers and can report with absolute confidence what they are hearing. For the first five days we make good progress; then Boxwell arrives to take over the running of our special training programme. Within hours Martingale runs foul of his new boss.

The tubby captain comes to sea with us in order to carry out an assessment inspection to see how well we have progressed. It consists of a series of exercises and evolutions ranging from torpedo attacks and gun action to seamanship and navigation. He feeds in all kinds of situations to catch the boat off-guard; even simulating the premature demise of the skipper to see how we cope without him. It is all good fun, but more reminiscent of prewar days; almost on the same level as a school sportsday, and Martingale grows more and more impatient as Boxwell ignores the true aim of our programme and has us running about like a lot of ODs in a training ship.

Things come to the boil when a lifejacket is hurled over the side so that we can practise 'man overboard' drill. In the midst of it all he orders, 'All non-swimmers muster on the after casing!'

It develops into chaos as Jumbo's men become mixed up with a crowd of extra bodies as they try to retrieve the life-jacket, with the result that the inevitable happens and we have to carry out a genuine rescue, and haul a half-drowned, spluttering stoker out of the sea.

Before we sail next morning for our normal exercise Martingale requests an interview with our new master and when he returns his face is set in an expression that shows only too clearly that the meeting was a disaster. Instinctively I know that we are in for a period of rebellion, and it starts that very evening when the H–boat signals that she has had enough and is returning to base. It should be our cue to follow her in, but not today. Martingale has been frothing at the mouth because we have been refused extra night exercises, so, after bidding the H–boat's surprised captain a curt goodbye, we turn away into the gathering gloom.

It is a blatant disregard for the routine set out by Boxwell, and just to compound the issue we send a diving signal and get below before we can receive an angry response from the depot ship. All through that long November night we prowl the Firth like a marauding shark, creeping up on anything that moves. Unsuspecting fishingboats and coasters that plod quietly through the protected waters are stalked as our lookouts sharpen up their night vision.

We carry out a few conventional attacks, piling on speed to get into an attacking position for a dived approach, but mainly we run in blind, with the Asdic team closed up as Trump and his men home us in with their ears. It is an exacting, difficult task. First the hydrophones locate a target, then the operators must listen to the beat of her screw and the pulse of her engine to determine whether they are listening to the slow beat of a merchantman's reciprocating engine, the smooth sound of turbines or the rattle of diesel. That tells us the type of vessel we are up against. It also provides the first indication of her course and speed as ranges and bearings are plotted on to the chart by the navigator. This is the moment when normally the skipper would use his periscope to obtain more accurate ranges and bearings. He would check her profile in the pages of *Jane's Fighting Ships* until he found her silhouette. Then by using the height of her mast he could establish her range.

Tonight we do it the hard way. It is entirely up to Trump to assess the stranger's identity, and the navigator to work out her movements from his chart. It is a matter of teamwork and experience, plus Martingale's imagination. It is also a risky, demanding occupation that could go dangerously wrong if they are not on the ball, for we could be on a collision course with any of those innocent quarries. Only a skilled operator can distinguish the sound of the target from background noises, and it takes a steady nerve to report with complete self-assurance.

If this was a submarine we were stalking we would switch to Asdic now, probing the depths with its incessant pings until it located the source of the sound. At first it would be a wide beam, allowing little definition, and it is down to the operator to bring us into its centre and run down towards the very core of the rebounding echoes as the supersonic pulses lance out from the oscillator. The quality of the sound will tell us the attitude of the enemy boat and what it is doing in relation to our own movements. It is second best to the real thing, and Martingale is hoping that the H–boat will give us a run for our money when she comes out to resume exercises before dawn tomorrow.

Submarine versus submarine is an evenly matched contest: almost man to man. However, in a real fight we will have the edge on the other boat. Trump's counterpart will be listening to our screws approaching, and her skipper will assume us to be a friend. Unfortunately, our Asdic can tell us everything except how deep she is, and Martingale must make a guess at that before he can order the settings on the torpedoes. Germans work in metres, and thirty metres will put the U–boat at just over ninety feet; deep enough to get away from the ocean swell, yet not too deep to surface quickly.

If he guesses it correctly we can hope for one out of a salvo of four torpedoes to hit the target, and the lucky U–boat men won't even hear the bang when the hull implodes on them. The unlucky ones are those who remain alive long enough to see the inexorable wall of water rushing in at them. They will die a gasping, struggling, screaming death as they feel their boat breaking up before it slips into its final dive.

If he gets it wrong we still have another four tubes standing by for another go, but Trump's opposite number will feel his heart grow cold when he hears a new sound above that of our diesels. A high-pitched whine that sends the fear of God through a man as it lances into his brain. He will try to control his voice as he makes his report, and his skipper will alter course in an effort to align his boat with the tracks of the torpedoes. The words will spread through the hull and freeze the men at their stations. In those few, agonisingly slow seconds they will grip their controls, stare hard at the thin metal hull, and die a thousand deaths before they hear them pass harmlessly by. The German skipper will be thinking hard. Should he go deep to complete his reloading, or surface to fight it out? According to the men we spoke to in *U–570*, it goes against the grain for many commanders to dive when under attack, for it leaves them vulnerable as they creep along at walking pace while the escorts home in on them with their Asdic pinging away. If it is at all possible they prefer to fight it out on the surface, and that is what we must assume.

So, the tiny coaster becomes a surfaced U–boat, struggling to overcome the inertia of a standing start after she has popped up from below. *Tarantula* broaches with her 4-inch manned and Martingale already bending over his night-sight, and two unassuming blokes in the small wheelhouse of the lonely little 'puffer' come close to having a heart attack.

After that the night passes quickly and uneventfully, and an hour or so before dawn finds us swimming in towards the channel to wait for the outward-bound H–boat. We are running on the electric motors to cut down noise while the look-outs use their ears and eyes to search the darkness ahead for the first sign of the 'enemy'. The question is, will the H–boat's captain play Martingale's game, or will he hold stringently to his set course in obedience to his orders?

I am on the bridge helm with the shadowy figures of the bridge party grouped around me. There is an air of tension as we move in like a ghost ship with the wind whining through the periscope standards. Aloft, on their raised platforms the look-outs are concentrating on their arcs with total commitment.

The night is as black as pitch, with just the odd patch of slate-grey showing between the clouds. We cannot see the shore, although we can sense its loom only five or six miles away. The wheel kicks now and again when we meet a cross-current or an eddy. The wind scuffs a cupful of spray inboard to wet the casing, but mostly the night is cold and silent.

The navigator gasps as he catches his breath and I snap a glance at him. He is poised with his binoculars focused on a bearing just off the port bow. He opens his mouth to speak when one of the lookouts beats him to it. 'I think I can 'ear somefink, sir!'

The wind blusters for a moment while we strain our ears. 'Are you certain?' asks Martingale softly.

A second's doubtful silence, then. 'Yes, sir. I'm sure I 'eard somefink. It sounds like an ex'aust. It came from somewhere across the bow, but I've lorst it.'

'I heard it too,' confirms the navigator. 'I think it came from close on the port bow.'

'Stop both!' Martingale's urgent order is a harsh whisper, and the boat loses way to wallow with the soft slop of her bilges taking over from the swish of her wash.

We curse the gusting wind as it moans through the standards. The sea sounds seem to grow as we strain our ears to listen. The night seems full of noise. How can we hear anything against that? The helm is useless, so I peer out into the blackness with the others. Shadows materialise into solid shape in my imagination, until I am on the point of reporting them, only to see them fade into nothing, so that I am left with the shadows once again.

'In both engine clutches!' orders the skipper.

'There it is!' shouts a look-out urgently, disregarding his formal training in his excitement.

The guttural mutter of exhausts lifts above the sea-noises for a moment so that we all hear it, and a sudden deep fear runs through my body.

'Sir! The hydrophones have picked up fast diesel,' calls Subby from the voicepipe. 'There is too much background noise to be certain, but they estimate red one oh.'

'Very good!' comes the standard reply in a tight voice.

'There it is!' It is a day for undisciplined reports, and this time it comes from the signalman, who should know better. 'I can hear it distinctly now.'

'Submarine dead ahead!' shouts another voice. 'She's comin' straight at us!'

A cold hand grabs at my heart at the sight of her ploughing in towards us with a bone in her teeth. 'Half ahead port –

starboard thirty!'

I spin the wheel as the telegraphs ring. The diesels jump into life as she fights to come round. He is bringing her bow towards the oncoming boat, and the distance between us is being swallowed up fast.

'Switch on the navigation lights!' yells Martingale. 'Half ahead together – wheel amidships – meet her – steady as she goes!'

Steady on zero four five, sir!' I respond automatically, forcing myself to ignore the other boat as I concentrate on the repeater. Our siren blares once to tell her we are swinging to starboard, and we pray that she holds on to her course to pass down our port side. There is an answering four blasts from the H–boat. 'Get out of my way!' she is shouting, 'I can't get out of yours!'

We career past each other with feet to spare, our wakes merging in confusion between the two hulls as pale faces peer back from her bridge. The first grey streaks of a new day are edging the ridge of distant hills as *Tarantula* comes about in a tight turn. The revolutions remain high as we range up alongside the other boat. 'It's Boxwell!' exclaims someone as we all recognise the plump figure amongst their bridge party.

'Stand by with your aldis!' orders Martingale calmly as the H–boat's lamp begins to blink.

'*HEAVE TO – I AM COMING ACROSS!*' spells out Bunts as he punctuates every word with an answering clack on his trigger.

After a few further exchanges the escorting trawler blusters up to lower a boat to ferry Boxwell over to us. He is no athlete, and when he arrives alongside he makes a hash of scrambling over our tanks. Jumbo is not noted for his gentle qualities, so Boxwell has little chance of making a dignified entrance as he is hoisted bodily onto the casing and sent sprawling. More willing hands reach down to stop him rolling back over the side; grabbing fistfuls of clothing to heave him inboard like a bundle of washing. He huff and puffs with his cap askew and his face a dangerous shade of crimson.

He ignores Martingale's salute to blunder aft to the footholds in the side of the bridge, and climbs up with a series of grunts to collapse into a quivering heap beside the 'pig's ear'. It has been quite a performance and I can see that some of the men have difficulty holding their features straight.

'You have gone too far this time,' he blusters when he gets his breathing back to somewhere near normal, as the skipper follows him up over the lip. 'You have no excuse for disregarding my orders. Only good fortune prevented a tragic accident this morning, and we could have lost two valuable submarines, not to mention their crews.'

He straightens his jacket and draws himself fully upright. 'I shall make it my duty to see that this farce is brought to an end once and for all. I have already voiced my concern to Captain S/M and Rear Admiral Plenty, and I can assure you that this little episode will ensure that *Tarantula* resumes her normal duties at once. As for your future: that depends very much on the final inspection which I intend to make tomorrow.'

He makes no attempt to lower his voice, even though every man on the bridge can hear his slating the skipper. 'You will undergo a full day's evolutions, and I will submit a report, along with my recommendations to Flag Officer Submarines. It will help them to make up their minds to discontinue this bloody pantomime and put this boat where she belongs, in an area where she can do the job for which she was designed, and not to play silly buggers at the whim of a jumped-up hot-head!'

His tone has risen with every word until he is wheezing with the strain. We watch him struggling to recover before he continues in a more moderate tone. 'Now, let us get on with the exercise. Give me five minutes to compose myself, then dive the boat.' He disappears through the upper hatch, leaving behind a stony silence.

'There is a place and means for every man alive,' quotes Falstaff glumly.

'Something is rotten in the state of Denmark,' responds Subby.

'Shut up, and get to your diving stations!' growls the skipper.

Next morning Boxwell puts us through the mill. No one relaxes for a single moment as he feeds in all kinds of emergencies and battle conditions. At one time we are under attack by two determined destroyers, Martingale and the first lieutenant are badly wounded, and Subby is in sole command. To his credit he is a level-headed youngster, and copes well, but the moment he solves one problem Boxwell comes up with a new one; each more devastating than the last.

'You have a depth-charge lodged in the casing,' shouts the tormentor. 'What are you going to do about it?'

'I've already done it, sir. Have I your permission to run to the heads?'

No one can win. When we carry out mock attacks on the trawler, Martingale is criticised for keeping the periscope exposed too long, then as we do another run in the afternoon he is condemned for not using it enough. Boxwell tears the boat apart, from the state of the crew's rig to the wardroom cutlery. The fact that we break all records when we reload the torpedo tubes, and the first round from our 4-inch demolishes the target, makes no impression, and he slangs the skipper in front of us all in a way that I wouldn't use on an OD in front of his mates.

It embarrasses everyone, but if he thinks it will undermine the skipper's prestige he is very much mistaken, for the more he rants and raves the more they rally round Martingale. If Boxwell was not so wrapped up in his personal vendetta he would only need to look at the faces of the men to see their resentment and feel their empathy.

Nonetheless, by the end of the day we are exhausted. Every man has had more than enough, and the boat herself seems to heave a heavy sigh of relief when the bumptious captain finally stumps across the plank to climb the long ladder to the depot ship's well-deck. Not without a parting shot, however. We are confined to harbour next day, and the boat will be cleaned throughout in time for a further inspection in the afternoon. The long list of items he has condemned ensures that no one will get ashore tonight.

His heels have hardly disappeared before the skipper calls a meeting in the wardroom. It consists of all heads of departments, and he spells out his intentions while we listen in growing concern, not for ourselves, but for him. If there was an award for sticking your neck out Martingale would win it hands down. Falstaff and Jumbo are to get the lads working like slaves on Boxwell's list, polishing and scrubbing until she gleams like a new pin, while the skipper goes ashore to make a series of telephone calls, including one to Rear Admiral Plenty. He must know that he will be putting many noses out of joint when he goes over Boxwell's head, but it makes no difference. He is determined to have one more go at getting permission for more night exercises, and pushing ahead with his ideas. The navy doesn't take kindly to junior officers who over-ride their senior officers, but despite Falstaff's warning not to sail too close to the wind, he goes ahead.

We are doing our best for him. Even Boxwell is unable to find anything to criticise when he completes his second inspection of the boat. He stalks like an avenging angel through the three ranks of our lads as they are drawn up in their 'number ones' on the depot ship's upper deck, staring into their faces as though he suspects each one of them of undermining his authority. In the end he has to accept that he cannot find fault, and with a brief salute, gives a grunt of frustration, and strides off to seek solace with a large, pink gin.

We need not have bothered as far as Martingale is concerned, for he seems determined to run foul of everyone as he disregards protocol and condemns himself in the eyes of his fellow officers who are steeped in a tradition that says that it is bad form to leap over the heads of senior officers. They were not present at the meeting when he put his case to the board, and in their eyes he is breaking all the rules for his own obsession.

More importantly from my point of view is the way he is alienating some of *Tarantula*'s company as they see their efforts virtually ignored. It is part of my job to be a buffer between officers and ratings, and to report to Falstaff if I believe that their confidence is being undermined. They can admire a man who sticks to his guns when he has a genuine cause, but after the near-collision with the H–boat some are convinced that he has shot his bolt, and going beyond all reason with his pig-headedness.

When he returns to the boat he barely responds to the trot–sentry's salute and rampages through the accommodation compartment like a wild bull until he finds me. 'You say that you are friendly with that Wren secretary in Boxwell's office, Grant. Do you really think that she is on our side?'

I look at him suspiciously. 'She is on your side, sir. I don't think she would be disloyal.'

'Have it your own way,' he snaps. 'I wouldn't dream of

asking her to do anything improper. The point is that it would be a help to know if there are still any of the local big-wigs who are not against my ideas. Tomorrow morning Captain Boxwell will be busy chasing Captain S/M and others in the depot ship with his complaints and recommendations; you can depend on that. Therefore, he will be out of his office for most of the morning. It would be a chance to have a word with her to find out if there is any influential senior officer who would be sympathetic to my project. Quite honestly, Grant, I am clutching at straws, and I cannot afford to miss a trick.'

I turn away. There is something here that I don't like. Like him, I know that Boxwell is an overstuffed, bigoted bastard who will stoop to any length to get his way, but that doesn't mean we should sink to his level, and this seems to be getting close to it. Martingale is talking about exploiting the friendship of a rather special person, and I don't want to be party to it. He is so determined to win, he is losing sight of basic ethics, and willing to sacrifice anyone for the cause.

'It might be better if you see her yourself, sir,' I say impassively. 'I have no excuse for going into Boxwell's office, and I might even get her into trouble if I do.'

'Nonsense! I haven't time to go myself. Don't you realise that the whole thing could be killed stone dead if we don't act quickly?'

'I know that, sir. Nevertheless, I am unhappy about doing this.'

He leans in closer. 'This is our last chance, Ben,' he pleads, using my Christian name to press it home. 'You and I have stuck our fingers into the fire before now. I can give you a document or two to make your visit official. You are a discreet sort of man; use your diplomacy. Remember, I am depending on you.'

I feel slightly sick, but I find myself agreeing. Maybe it is just a secret yearning to see her again. 'I won't do anything to jeopardise her career, sir.'

He gets angry. 'Damn it, man! Who's asking you to? Do you think I have no scruples?' He slams a hand down hard on the mess-table. 'I am not going to order you to do anything that goes against your conscience. Are you going or not?'

I look into his eyes. 'Yes, sir, I'll go.'

Three

In prewar days Boxwell's office was part of a refined private hotel that boasted excellent sea views and a quiet atmosphere. Now it also serves as living quarters for some of his senior staff, although he prefers to occupy more opulent rooms in one of the grander hotels on the seafront. He divides his time between the offices and the depot-ship, and most of the everyday business is left in the capable hands of an angular, schoolmarmish second officer, who looks on anyone below the rank of commander as peasantry. On the ground floor a general office occupies the ex-dining room and lounge, and the reception desk still serves the same purpose with one major difference. Where once guests were welcomed with a smile a well-selected corps of dragons stand by to repel boarders. No one gets past this outpost without a cast iron reason to penetrate the upper sanctum where Boxwell's personal offices are situated. When I stroll in with a face-full of confidence it is rapidly demolished by a stoney-faced Wren manning the barricade, while her haughty superior stands aloof in the background.

I wave a large, buff envelope at her, and she wrinkles her nose disdainfully. 'Yes?' she demands, eyeing me up and down as though I should be hanging in a butcher's window.

Her tone, and a sharp glance from the paragon in the background, put me on my guard. 'Captain Boxwell's office please,' I ask in what I hope is a disarming voice.

'Have you an appointment?'

'More or less.'

'What is that supposed to mean?' There is a quickening interest in the officer's expression. 'Captain Boxwell is not in at the moment, and even if he was he sees no one without an appointment, least of all a rating. You may leave the envelope with me.'

I snatch it close to my chest as though it contains top secret papers. 'I know he isn't here,' I lie. 'I have strict instructions to hand this to his personal secretary, and I have a verbal message too. I am the coxswain of HM Submarine *Tarantula*. Captain Boxwell inspected the boat yesterday, and I have been given these to deliver.' It's not too far from the truth when I think about it: I *have* been sent, and he *did* inspect the boat; it's up to her how she puts the two together.

It cuts no ice with her. 'I am sure no one will object if you leave that with me,' she insists with a deadly smile.

'Sorry, marm. I can't do that. If I cannot carry out my orders I must return to the boat and tell my captain.' I look as donkeybrained as possible.

'What is your name?' Her voice holds a threat as she edges the receptionist aside to confront me.

I return her stare without blinking. 'Chief Petty Officer Grant, marm.'

She is unimpressed. 'You are extremely obdurate, chief. You must know full well that it is perfectly in order for you to leave those documents with me.'

'No, marm,' I state stolidly. 'If I can't deliver them to Captain Boxwell's secretary personally I must go back and report to my captain.'

Her steely eyes dart down to the desk for a second. 'I shall do a little reporting of my own if you don't comply, Chief Petty Officer Grant. I do not pretend to know what this is all about, nor do I believe for one moment that you are as mule-headed as you make out.' She reaches for a telephone, presses a switch and winds a handle. 'Ask Leading Wren Wellington to come down into reception,' she orders, then replaces the receiver as though it is unclean.

She comes in looking even more fresh and delectable than I remember, and doesn't bat an eyelid when she sees me standing there, but turns towards the desk where two pairs of suspicious eyes are watching carefully. 'Yes, ma'am?'

'You have a visitor. A rating from HMS *Tarantula* who refuses to leave his message with anyone other than Captain

Boxwell's secretary. Find out what he wants and then get rid of him.' She makes me feel like a rodent.

There is a large bay window near the main door that forms a small alcove with a window-seat and a coffee-table. Relics from the past by the look of them. I place the envelope on the table when she invites me to sit beside her. We make a fine pair of conspirators as we sit with our knees very close together. 'These are to be filed, and I have a message from Lieutenant-Commander Martingale with the timetable for tomorrow's exercises.' I allow my voice to fall away as I speak, as though I consider what I have to say confidential, and the two women raise their eyebrows in mutual looks of derision. They have accepted that I must be more wooden-headed than I appear: a knuckle-brained subordinate with no mind of his own.

I am beginning to founder though. For one thing, sitting as close to her as this has a disarming effect on me, and throws my self confidence askew, and I wonder if Martingale realises what a lucky sod he is. I desperately need to get her away from here, out of range of those penetrating glares.

I should not have worried, for this girl has far sharper wits than I have. 'You could easily have told all this to Second Officer Metcalf,' she exclaims in a loud, admonishing voice, bringing looks of smug satisfaction from our audience. 'I will jot down the times and details.'

She takes out a small notepad and writes. 'Meet me in front of the public library in thirty minutes.' Then she slips out the page and hands it to me. 'There's your copy. Make certain your commanding officer gets it.' She speaks as though she is trying to get a message through to an idiot.

I assume a suitably hangdog expression and slope out beneath the superior noses of the reception committee. Outside the wind is scuffing up loose paper and driving spray across the guard rails. I can see *Tarantula* snuggling up tight against the depot ship, with a smaller boat moored alongside her. It is a bleak, sombre day, with the promise of a winter storm. I smile to myself as I recall how adeptly she coped with the situation. How she weighed things up so quickly amazes me. She was brilliant, but I have a twinge or two of conscience when I think of the sour features of the other two. It pleased them both to see me taken down a peg, but if they ever realise how they have been taken for a ride, heaven help Leading Wren Wellington.

Smack on time she comes trotting along with her hair tucked up tidily under her cap and a heavy overcoat buttoned right up to the neck. We stroll along together until we find a small, chintzy cafe with paper doyleys set out on starchy, white covers. Wartime fare has restricted the menu, but what there is is home-baked. We settle for tea and scones, with a scrape of margarine.

'I half expected you,' she says quietly, 'but I didn't expect you to play the errand-boy.'

I toy with my scone and study the willow-patterned plate. 'You know my name. What do I call you?'

'Laura.'

'Well, Laura. We are in dead trouble. To keep it short, our last exercise was a bit of a shambles and unless something pretty drastic turns up all the skipper's plans will go to pot.' I look at her, slightly miffed. 'And I am not an errand-boy.'

She smiles ruefully. 'No. I'm sorry. That was unfair. I know more about what goes on than you realise, and I can well understand how desperate he must be feeling, but I don't see how I can possibly help.'

'Right now he is telephoning everyone up to the Pope to see if he can find some support for his scheme, and that's where you come in. We wondered if you know anyone locally with enough gold-braid who might put up an argument on his behalf. To be perfectly honest, Laura, unless some sort of miracle turns up, I don't give a toss for his chances.'

She looks at me with an old-fashioned expression. 'So you thought that I might be persuaded to part with a few trade secrets?' There is an edge to her voice, and I feel another twinge.

'Not exactly. Just a name would do. After all, you did warn us about Boxwell.'

'And whose idea was this? As if I didn't know!'

'Is that important?'

'It is to me. Do you know why I am in this job, Ben?' The intense way she is looking into my eyes has me shuffling about uncomfortably. 'Because I have a reputation for being discreet. Now you are asking me to betray that trust and disclose confidential business. What would you call someone who does that?'

'We are not asking for more than a name.'

'You keep saying "we". I know who is at the back of all this, and you can tell your worthy captain that I am not in the habit of disclosing what I overhear in the course of my duties for him or anyone. You can also tell him to do his own dirty work in future, and not embarrass other people.'

'It is not like that at all,' I protest weakly. 'You said yourself that I am not just an errand-boy. We don't want you to do anything that goes against your conscience. He thinks too much of you for that, believe me.'

'Does he? I can see now that I made a mistake when I told you about Boxwell's appointment. I liked the look of you both, and I thought all the big guns were loaded against you, but that doesn't mean that I am your inside agent. I don't know why he is so obsessed with this scheme of his. Perhaps it is about time that he came down to earth and realised that the navy is not run entirely for his benefit. I know that you were put up to it, Ben, but I also know that you are not a stupid man. You must have known that it was wrong to ask this.'

'He is clutching at straws,' I plead lamely.

She sets her cup down firmly. 'Hard luck! He will do anything, and use anyone to achieve his goal. Like me, you are just a pawn.' She sighs and looks at me in quiet submission. 'Like me, you like the man, and will do almost anything to help him beat the system. It is a little one-sided, don't you think?' She sighs again. 'All right, I will give you a name: Lieutenant Matthew Cumber. He is the captain of the training boat. He and Boxwell had words together yesterday, and from the snippet I heard it seems that the near collision was not entirely unplanned. They knew where you were, and Cumber wanted to sheer off, but Boxwell wanted to teach you a lesson. You were never in any danger, but nevertheless the lieutenant told Boxwell in no uncertain terms what he thought of him. So you see, someone else has fallen into the Martingale trap.' She rises out of her chair and looks down at me. 'There now. You have got what you came for. I hope that Lieutenant-Commander Richard Martingale is duly obliged. I am going to leave you to settle this bill; I think it is appropriate, don't you?'

She spins on her heels and stalks out of the cafe. The wind catches her as she steps out onto the pavement and she has to brace up against it. In spite of it she holds her head up high as she walks along the front; proud and dignified.

*

A lot has gone on since I went ashore. A long fuel-pipe is pulsing away as it fills our tanks, and all the polish and bullshit has disappeared beneath a mess of incoming stores and ammunition. The boat takes on a more warlike appearance as the lads go about preparing her for sea. Boxwell would have a fit if he could see how quickly *Tarantula* converts back into a ship of war. The scrubbed tables are hoisted up and locked into place on the deckhead to make way for a new lot of torpedoes; this time with the red-painted warheads fitted. Clump's great oily boots, and those of his mates are making a hell of a mess on the shiny cortecined deck. It is a sort of organised chaos as everyone humps things about, and I find Jumbo helping to rig the torpedo-loading rails. 'What the hell is going on?' I ask.

'Christ knows! The depot ship piped "*Tarantula*'s ship's company to report to their boat" about an hour ago. Since then it's bin nothin' but sweat. Looks like we're finished playin' silly buggers though.'

'Where's Falstaff?'

'Dahn below with the gunlayer; they're stowing ammunition.'

I make my way down through the conning-tower and find them in the control room with the magazine hatch gaping as the men pass 4-inch rounds through to their mates below.

'Ah, Grant!' says Falstaff when he sees me hovering in the background. 'Sudden panic, I'm afraid. We have to be ready for sea by sixteen hundred, and I'd like you to check that we have enough grub on board for a twenty-one day patrol.'

'Aye aye, sir.' The why's and wherefore's will have to come later if I am to argue with the depotship's "jack dusties" to make sure we get our full quota of the best they have in stock. In particular I want ultra fresh vegetables with no blemishes, so that they won't turn rotten quickly in the fetid atmosphere of the boat.

By three-thirty the boat is ready, and when Falstaff and I

make a final inspection of all compartments we find little to complain about, and Jumbo has all his shorelines singled up ready for slipping when the skipper makes his appearance at five minutes to sailing time. He snaps a hasty salute as Falstaff reports the boat ready, and grunts an order to ring down 'stand by!' to the motor room. I glance up to where the huge flank of the depotship seems to lean out over us, and there is Boxwell's round face beaming smugly down at Martingale. Even from this distance I can see the look of triumph in his eyes.

Without fuss we back up on the spring to angle the bow out, then slide easily out of the depot ship's shadow and into the main channel. The main engines take over from the motors as we point our bow towards the open sea. Bunts blows one blast on his whistle, and the thin reply comes drifting across from the other ship. It is our final farewell, and already the crew is stowing away the last hawser as the first slop of open water splatters over them.

'Patrol routine!' orders Martingale. 'I want you in the wardroom, Grant.'

'Aye aye, sir.' This is unusual; he likes to remain on the bridge until we are well clear of the Firth as a rule. The helmsman takes over in the control room, and I clatter down into the muggy warmth to find him waiting for me in the wardroom on his own.

'Well?' he demands, glaring at me.

I stare back at him, puzzled. 'Sir?'

'You know damned well what I want to know! Did you find out anything from Laura?'

For a moment I choke over my answer. 'Surely there is no point in going over that now, sir?'

'That is for me to decide.' He slops whisky into a glass and swigs it back. 'I repeat: Did you find out anything?'

'She mentioned an argument between the captain of the H–boat and Boxwell, sir. She only caught part of it, but it sounded as though the H–boat could have avoided a near miss if her skipper had been allowed to have his way.'

He knocks back another tot and bangs the glass down hard on the table. 'Good girl! I knew she would come up with something.' He looks away for a moment. There is something nasty in the way he is behaving today, and I have never known him drink at sea before. 'Makes sense when you think about it. Boxwell up to his bloody tricks. We assumed the wind was causing the sound of her engine to lift and fade like that. What if she was shutting down every so often to use her hydrophones? She had the edge on us too, because we had a background of surf from the shore to contend with, while all she had was open water, except for Ailsa Craig. I wouldn't put it past Boxwell to risk a near collision to prove his point.'

I shuffle uncomfortably. 'Well it is all academic now, isn't it, sir? Not much point in pushing it further. You might even get Laura into a lot of bother if they put two and two together. There was a starchy Wren officer in Boxwell's office, just waiting to land us in the soup if she gets half a chance. If she ever found out that she's been taken for a ride she'll throw the book at Laura, and enjoy every minute of it.' I try to change the subject. 'Did you have any luck with your 'phone calls?'

'That was a mistake,' he says in a disgruntled voice. 'Senior officers stick together. They take exception to subordinates trying to over-ride one of their own kind. I should have known better. It was foolish; I can see that now. I allowed my frustration to get the better of me. I spoke to Rear Admiral Plenty, and for a moment I thought he was on my side again, but I was wrong; he was only being non-committal. All I succeeded in doing was set them all against me. I am considered to be an ill-mannered, insubordinate lout, who needs to be taken down a peg or two: a pain in the arse. They've closed ranks on me.'

'Well, it looks as though it has been taken out of our hands now, sir.'

He glares at me. 'Give up, you mean? Christ, Grant, I thought I could depend on you for support!'

I gape at him incredulously. 'The work-up is over, sir. Surely that's the end of it?'

'Not for me it isn't,' he declares forcefully. 'Don't worry, Grant, I shan't get you or Laura into bother.'

Now it is my turn to become shirty. 'That's the last thing we're concerned about, and well you know it – sir.' I snap the last word out viciously. 'What upsets me is that you don't seem to have any scruples about using her.'

His face hardens. 'That's enough! Have you no work to be getting on with?'

'Yes, sir,' I say bitterly. 'I've got things to do.'

'Well, bloody well get on with it, and stop pontificating like a supercilious sin-bos'n.'

That does it. I slide out with my rage boiling inside. There is no excuse for that. Before I get to my mess the shout comes from the control room. 'Captain to the bridge!' I hear his feet go clattering up the ladder.

For a while I try to concentrate on some paperwork, but in the end I have to give up on it and ask permission to go up top. I feel the need to get out of the stodgy warmth and into the fresh air for a while. The sun is lighting the shoreline astern as we run clear of the land, and Jumbo is finishing off his inspection of the after casing with Subby at his heels. They will be checking to make certain that every rope and hawser is well secured and that there is nothing to rattle about under there that will give us away when we are trying to run silent under the surface.

Martingale and Falstaff are in a huddle at the fore-end of the bridge, and when they notice me standing behind them I am ordered to take over the bridge helm. 'Follow the trawler,' the skipper says, as though our little altercation has never taken place.

I look ahead at the squat stern of our escort and spin the wheel to line up our bow with it. She is leading us out through the swept channel, and the boat is falling into our normal patrol routine naturally as we catch the first real swell of the open sea, with the Isle of Arran to starboard and Pladda Light ahead. The first long shadows of night are closing in to turn the silhouetted shapes on the bridge steel grey, and the wind takes on a chill that drives down into my bones. A shiver runs through me as the last, persistent gull makes a final soaring arc above the periscope standards before turning shorewards to find a roost on the purple cliffs.

There is a lamp blinking through the dusk from the trawler as she bids us farewell, and hauls off to starboard to make her run back home. She leaves behind a lonely, melancholy ocean as we switch back to the control room steering, and I take one last, lingering look at the olive sea before going down into the snug warmth of the boat where red watch has taken over from the 'harbour stations' crowd. There is no further use for me on the helm, so I slide into the chiefs' mess in time for the evening meal. No sooner am I sat than the tannoy crackles into life.

'This is the captain. I expect that you are eager to know where we are going so I won't keep you in suspense any longer. Our first stop is Gibraltar, and then it's on into the Mediterranean. We have been ordered to make as much speed as possible, because our chums out there are having a busy time trying to stop supplies getting through to the Afrika Korps. We will be going on to Malta with a cargo of vital spare parts for some of the boats already there, but eventually we shall be based at Alexandria. Those of you who know her will be glad to learn that *Medway* is to be our depot ship. Those of you don't know her will soon come to realise that she is the best of the bunch. In fact there are some of us who believe that the navy had a brainstorm when they commissioned her, for she knows how to treat submariners, and is not just a floating barracks like some others we know.'

He takes a short pause before going on in a more serious voice. 'This is not what we trained for, and some of you might be disappointed at being prevented from putting all our hard training into practice. However, I can assure you that the project is far from dead. The moment the opportunity comes I intend to prove that our scheme can be a success. In the meantime, keep your eyes skinned when you are on look-out, for we are in a hurry, and I do not wish to dive more than absolutely necessary. That's all!'

I have my head against the bulkhead that separates our mess from the wardroom, and I hear a murmur of conversation as I ponder over his words. As always it is Falstaff who sums things up with one of his quotes. ''Tis now the very witching time of night, when churchyards yawn and hell itself breathes out contagion.'

'Cheerful bastard!' snipes the bloke sitting next to me as he digs his fork into his stew.

Four

This is when *Tarantula* is at her best, when she throws off the cloying embrace of the land and thrusts her lean shape through the sea. She was not designed to ride the oceans, but to become part of it. Those who control our destiny have decided that we will get on much faster if we travel alone. However, to travel fast a submarine must remain surfaced and use her diesels. The snag is the volatile stretch of water between the English coast and the 'Rock', which is one gigantic battlefield, with everyone at one another's throat. U–boats gang up in wolf-packs to attack slow-moving convoys, and escorts plaster anything that resembles a submarine.

From Admiralty signals we know that the Germans are shadowing a northbound convoy, and that support groups are running down contacts in the area. There is an auxiliary aircraft-carrier there too; one of those conversion jobs with half a dozen Martlets and a lot of optimism. Her aircraft are mainly involved with driving away the big Kondors that like to sit over a convoy and call up Dönitz's boys for the slaughter. We try to give it all a wide berth, but it is a long way round and we are in a hurry, so it is a compromise as we thunder along at full speed on the fringe.

When we are forced down by sightings, false or otherwise, we learn the art of creeping along in stealthy silence, passing orders in heavy whispers, with all movement restricted. Any man who has the temerity to request the use of the heads receives a frown and a curt refusal, for there is a complicated drill with a lot of noisy compressed air, and you learn to regulate your bodily functions in boats.

Martingale insists on absolute silence, with all unnecessary machinery turned off as the long minutes tick by agonisingly slowly, with all our nerves stretched taut as piano-wire as we listen for the slightest sound. The thing you require at times like this is a lively imagination as she creeps through currents that run stealthy fingers along the hull.

Trump is our star performer. The virtuoso whose speciality is sound. His expert ears must be rested as much as possible, and Martingale ensures that he is kept in reserve for the moments when our future depends on what he hears, and how he interprets it. Tiredness or lack of oxygen after a long dive can dull a man's mind and make him hear things that are not there, and he must be trusted implicitly when our lives depend on his skill as we run blind under the water. Heaven help us if he begins to hallucinate.

With one motor shut down we creep along at 'dead slow', choking back our anxiety until Martingale deems it safe to go up to periscope depth to take a look. That is when we are most vulnerable, in those few moments when we are near the surface before the lens pokes up to see. We know only too well that other experts like Trump are listening too, every bit as adept as he is at deciphering what they hear over their earphones. The strain is continuous. Mouths go dry, insides cramp, and bellies churn. It affects you by degrees in the long periods of silence, when you try to avoid other men's eyes and bury your fear.

Eventually the skipper walks the periscope round, studying the sky and the sea, unwilling to trust his own eyes without checking and double-checking that small arc of vision, where every cloud hides a potential enemy who can appear seconds after the lens has swept by. It takes only a few seconds for an aircraft to dive in at two hundred knots with bomb-bay open and depth-charges primed.

We hold our breath and curb our imagination as he carries out one more meticulous examination before standing back and snapping his finger for the leading stoker manning the control lever to lower the periscope down into its well.

'Blow main ballast – surface!'

The high pressure air roars into the tanks and the hydroplanes go to 'rise'. The skipper climbs up into the conning tower and takes off the first clip, while Bunts watches from below, calling out the depth as we go up. At ten feet the second clip comes off and the hatch jumps back into its clamp as the pressure inside the boat forces it from its seating. A small cataract of water splashes over Martingale's shoulders as he climbs out onto the bridge.

The gunlayer is at the helm. He opens the valve on the bridge voice-pipe and catches a half a pint of water in a bucket as it drains down before the first orders come. Martingale will have made his final all-round check of sky and horizon.

'In both engine clutches – half ahead together – start the blowers!'

The diesels rumble into their steady melody and a cold blast breathes into the boat. The low pressure blowers pump air into the ballast tanks to give full buoyancy.

'Patrol routine – look-outs up!'

A thousand times we've done it, yet a sigh of relief runs through the boat as we stand down from 'diving stations' and a third of the crew take over the boat. Sweet fresh air pours into the hull and men begin to light cigarettes. The cook gets busy in his tiny galley. The boat rolls and lifts as she gathers speed. It seems that we have found a circle of blank ocean amid all the hell that is breaking loose in this part of the world.

I ask permission to go up top to look out at a rolling desert of grey/green hillocks stretching away to infinity with an occasional greyback to give it life. Beneath our keel the seabed must resemble a junkyard where broken ships lie with great holes in their sides and their expensive cargoes spilling out, while bodies with empty eye-sockets and bloated torsos dance a macabre ballet in the undulating swirls of cruel currents.

Reports of enemy movements come in more frequently as we travel southward. We are forced to dive three times during the forenoon, and eventually Martingale decides that it is time to conform to the standard practice of staying dived all through the day. Fortunately the November days are short, so the air stays reasonable and there is plenty of time to replenish the batteries at night.

Most boats get a 'soft patrol' as a sort of extra working-up period, but we are being denied this. So the crew must adapt quickly to patrol conditions as we plough out to the Med. The reports paint a picture of mayhem, with close escorts and support groups trying to protect their charges from marauding U-boats who are gathering in packs for a night attack.

Just before 'tot time', our PO telegraphist, reports that he is picking up transmissions every hour. A series of 'V's over a three minute period. We know that the boffins back home have broken German codes and learned what frequencies the U–boats use, although the enemy is unaware of it, and becomes extremely loquacious at times when they transmit on high frequency wavebands to Befehlshaber der Unterseeboote (BdU) with information as to their whereabouts, state of fuel, and details of the convoys they are shadowing. It never ceases to amaze us that they are so free with their radios; when we take such great care to maintain radio silence. Using High Frequency Direction finders our escorts can run down a radio beam and find a target at the end of it, while others work in pairs to obtain cross bearing and obtain good fixes on U–boats. Yet still the U–boat Command refuses to accept that the British can monitor their signals.

Today, however, the radio signals are on medium band and consist of only the series of 'V's. 'It must be a homing signal,' says Martingale. 'Have you a bearing on it?'

Sparks is a mournful sort of bloke and talks as though each sentence is his last. 'Only an approximate one, sir. I estimate a bearing of around green one five. The strength is good, so I would say no more than thirty miles away.'

The skipper moves across to the chart-table and taps thoughtfully with a pair of dividers. I sit with my back to the controls and dials of the hydroplanes with Jumbo beside me, both watching shamelessly as we eavesdrop. Apart from us, the helmsman, and the control room log-keeper, the only other person close by is the navigator who is peering over his master's shoulder.

'Do we know where that northbound convoy is at the moment?' asks the skipper.

The navigator points a long, bony finger at a spot on his chart. 'That's the last known position, sir. At seven knots they can't have moved too far away in half an hour.'

'That puts the U–boat thirty miles away from the convoy,' muses the skipper. 'If she is shadowing she is certainly keeping her distance. Usually they stay ahead or slightly ahead of the beam, as opposed to following astern, because it puts them in a good attacking position when the time comes. Maybe this bloke is just being cagey until his mates are all assembled. He won't wish to lead them amongst the escorts, and on a clear day like this he should see the odd column of smoke from some struggling merchantman trying to keep up with the other ships, and of course there is always the good old Kondor to keep a bird's eye view on things.' He taps harder. 'No, he's our boy all right. He's the one who is leading the rest into the fray.'

The navigator has pushed past to draw in his lines of predicted courses. 'We should pass right down between the convoy and the U–boat if we stay on one eight zero, sir. I must remind you that we are already four hundred miles west of Cape Finisterre, and should be thinking of altering to the east.'

'How accurate are your bearings, Sparks?'

Jennings's face lengthens, and his voice is even more funereal than normal as he mutters, 'Not bad, sir. If the U–boat sticks to its time-table we should get another fix in about twenty minutes. That will confirm it.' There is no emotion in his voice. It is as though he is making a routine weather report as he stares into the distance.

'There could be a whole swarm of the sods in that area,' snorts the navigator.

'On the other hand, they have no idea that *Tarantula* is in the area,' says Martingale thoughtfully. 'They will expect any boat that comes along to be one of their own.'

'So will our lot, sir,' warns the navigator soberly. 'If we can pick up the transmissions, so can they, and one submarine is much like another when you are chasing down a radio-beam with the depth-charge crews closed up. We could run into a bloody hornet's nest.'

'That depends on how keen they are to weaken the screen. They may consider thirty miles too far to chase after a radio signal that could turn out to be a decoy.'

They stand silent for a moment while Jennings fidgets with his backside on the fringe. 'We'll get another opinion,' asserts Martingale. 'Let's ask the Bard.'

Falstaff is in the wardroom, preparing to go on watch, and wearing red glasses to get his eyes adjusted while he sorts out his standard bridge dress, which consists of a RAF flying-jacket, silk scarf, riding-breeches and boots. The only concession he makes to uniform is a battered cap with a tarnished badge.

'We have this blessed U–boat somewhere to the south of us, Number One,' says Martingale. 'Despite our orders to stay clear, I think it is too good an opportunity to miss. What say you?'

Falstaff lifts his head and adopts his best thespian tone. 'Though this be madness, yet there is method in't. A man can die but once, and we owe God a life.'

'What the hell's all that supposed to mean?' snaps the navigator.

'Let's go after the bastard!'

'Well, why the hell can't you say so in plain language,' grumbles Martingale.

'Aye, Captain!' blares Falstaff in his best sea-dog voice. 'I must away aloft and send down the ancient mariner himself. It will be good to get our teeth into something positive for a change, and Sub will want to check his torpedo firing equipment.' He places one foot on the ladder and waves an arm. 'It is bright day that brings forth the adder,' he roars, then goes blustering up against the eighty knot wind that funnels down the tower.

'Do you think we lesser mortals will ever understand the workings of such a superior mind?' asks the navigator as the noise subsides.

'I don't believe for one minute that he knows himself,' declares Martingale. 'One day he will be a pain in the arse to his own crew, like many captains I know who quote the bible all over the place, especially when signalling other ships. Most of the time their quotes are so obtuse they confuse everyone but themselves.' He studies the chart for a moment before looking into the navigator's face. 'I'll stay here and work out my plan of action. You go up top and tell Number One to alter course to one nine zero. We will try to get the moon behind that U–boat. I hope those Nazis are in a cocky mood tonight, and greet us as a long-lost brother.'

He turns to Jennings. 'Get back to your caboosh and monitor those signals. You should have plenty of time to obtain a good bearing if they play their part. Listen round on all bearings in case other boats start to respond. Let me know at once if they do, and note down the bearings yourself. Those boys can get most talkative when they are closing in for the kill – God bless their funny little ways!'

Now he turns to the gunlayer on the helm. 'Tell the first lieutenant to go full ahead on this course until further orders.'

Despite the unholy hour there is an air of expectancy running through the boat now. We have sneaked along like a scared rabbit for long enough, and most of us welcome the opportunity to become the aggressor for a change. There is always that little twinge of nerves of course. It grabs at your gut from time to time, but it sets the adrenalin going and sharpens up the mind. There has been one false alarm after another, and now at last it is the real thing. To say that we are looking forward to it would be crazy, but slinking along day after day, with the ever-present tension gnawing at your insides is no alternative to a bit of real action. For the first time we'll know how *Tarantula*'s untried company will react. No amount of drill or simulated exercises can compensate for the real thing.

In a few hours we will know who can or who cannot be trusted; and that applies not only to the new hands. Some of the veterans have seen a lot of action and known a lot of stress. Their minds and bodies have been tested over and over, and I have noticed fists clenching white-knuckled from time to time when a report sends us scuttling below. They know the awful, mind-numbing detonations of depth-charges, and the way a man's stomach churns at the sound of propellers driving overhead as a boat tries to wriggle off the hook, and I'm certainly not immune. I have that same nausea in my guts at times.

Experience is an advantage most times, but it can also be a menace when it plays on a man's imagination. They say that knowledge is the antidote to fear. The snag is that when a boat is under attack there is nothing to see, and all the indescribable noises come from outside the hull. It requires imagination to interpret those sounds, and then imagination and reality become blurred.

The greatest fear of all is that you will break down in front of your mates, and the amazing thing is that very few do, and most acquit themselves well when the chips are down. No one ever knows that other bellies are revolving like their own, or that theirs are not the only nerves jumping every time an odd noise comes. When it is all over they will get that glowing sense of exhilaration that comes when they realise how well they have behaved.

In the meantime they must look to the older hands for guidance. Which brings an added burden to the senior men who must bury their own feelings beneath a façade of composure and self-assurance that belies what is going on inside. They know from experience that the sickness lasts only during the long period of waiting. Once things start to happen the fear will vanish. But knowing is one thing: living through it time and time again makes it harder to contain with each successive patrol. You put to the back of your mind statistics that tell you that the life expectancy of a submariner at this stage of the game is about forty days. All that means is that some will die today, while others, like you, will go on to survive the war. If you did not believe that you would go nuts. Self-preservation is the ultimate aim of everyone on both sides. It occupies the mind and focuses attention on the job.

'This is the captain!' Martingale's calm voice cuts into my thoughts, and every ear pricks up. 'You will be pleased to hear that the gods have been kind to us. Next to *Tirpitz* a nice, fat U–boat is as prime a target as we can get, and it looks like there's one of them trundling along to the south of us, tracking a northbound convoy. I have altered course and dropped our speed a little so that we can make our approach from the west at dawn, which should mean that she will be silhouetted against the rising sun when we come within range. In one hour we will go to diving stations and swop over to the main motors. That is all the time you have to get your coughing and sneezing over with, for once we get within hydrophone range I will personally castrate anyone who so much as breaks wind.'

He pauses for a moment to allow us to absorb his words, then goes on in lighter vein. 'I have told the chef to serve up a good breakfast. So, all you mess-cooks take eggs and bacon along to the galley and we will go into battle with our bellies full. As soon as you have eaten, clear away the debris and strip down the fore-ends for action. That's all.'

The tannoy clicks off, leaving an empty silence for a moment, then the hubbub erupts as they set about doing all that needs to be done before the appointed hour. I decide to use part of that time to take a stroll through the boat, testing the atmosphere and giving a word of reassurance here and there. If I were an outsider I would assume that the boat was going to a picnic, for there is plenty of ribald banter and good humour in the messes.

In the torpedo stowage compartment the tables and stools have already been cleared away, and all the domestic gear shoved through the bulkhead door into the accommodation area, for the torpedomen will need every inch of space to manipulate their one and a half ton missiles. Numbers one and two forward tubes are exterior ones and cannot be reloaded at sea, but that still leaves six others; two of which are below deck level. It means that deckboards have to be lifted to allow them to be loaded through two small, circular bulkhead doors. The remaining four are easier, but still require plenty of muscle and expertise to reload quickly. On a good day Tod Cooper, the torpedo gunner's mate, and his men can do the job in less than ten minutes, and they say the record stands at six, in ideal conditions, and under competitive circumstances.

Tod is a mild mannered, pink-skinned man, with startling blue eyes that match his well-bleached boilersuit, which is the envy of everyone. His secret is a mixture of soapflakes, 'pussers hard' soap and soda. Others have tried and watched their garments slowly disintegrate. There is something magical about them too, for they never seem to get dirty. Even now he is squeezed into the narrow alleyway between the banks of torpedo tubes, checking the indicators to make certain the bow-caps are shut, which would leave us lesser mortals begrimed with layers of shale-oil and grease. Not him: he will emerge spotless, wiping his hands on a wad of cotton waste.

His minions go about their duties with subdued, muttered remarks, only a proportion of which have anything to do with the job in hand. They are transforming the living quarters into a hard, metallic workshop to turn *Tarantula* into a guided missile launcher. Just as Nelson's men ripped their ships apart when they cleared for action, so these boys are pretty ruthless when it comes to items that have been left 'sculling' about by neglectful colleagues. There are many who would dearly love to follow the example of their eighteenth-century forebears and throw the officers' prize possessions overboard with gay abandon, and anyone who leaves his personal gear lying about gets no favours from them.

'Clump!' shouts a voice as a bucket whistles past my ear. 'Those dirty great clod-hoppers of yours are takin' up orl the space.'

'Big feet – big chopper, mate,' chides the youngster with a lecherous grin.

'It ain't the size that counts – it's the way yer wiggles it,' comments another.

There is not much wrong with the atmosphere here. A certain tension in the laughter that follows a pretty weak joke maybe, but that is to be expected.

Moving aft through the bulkhead I enter the least disrupted part of the boat, known laughingly as the accommodation compartment, for most of the ratings live and sleep in the fore-ends, while these messes are reserved for senior hands. Beneath my feet banks of batteries simmer away to produce power for the boat and her main motors. They need to be recharged regularly and kept dipped to ensure they stay in good condition. They occupy most of the space down there, but beneath them again there are fuel tanks and bottles containing another precious commodity – compressed air to purge the ballast-tanks when we surface. *Tarantula* requires feeding, watering, and servicing to function well, and it seems that the human beings required to perform those duties are the least considered in the minds of those who design boats like her. That is until you stop to consider how much has to be crammed into her slim, pressurised body.

Just two hundred and seventy feet, by twenty-six, by fourteen. At the widest part of her hull; amidships, two men of medium height can lie with their feet touching the sides and their arms overlapping above their heads. Not one inch is wasted. No extravagant luxury allowed. Not as spartan as the U-boat we are chasing after perhaps, but then the Germans seem to have an obsession with making life as basic as possible for their submariners.

Next to this compartment is the heart of the monster. It is also the largest, and contains the nerve centre that governs everything she does. Her eyes and ears are contained here when we are beneath the surface. The Asdic cabinet, radio cabin, wardroom, galley, heads, they are all situated between the two pressurised bulkheads, along with a whole mass of other things. The main area is dominated by the control room with its diving panel, hydroplane controls, helm, periscope, torpedo firing panels, chart-table and flood control box, along with the telegraphs and a thousand other controls that send out signals to the far ends of the boat.

From the hull itself grows a jungle of metallic flora, a mass of multi-coloured pipes and valves, cables and switches, that run through her length with supplies of fuel, water, air and power. All to be allotted their space in the overcrowded, complicated body. It is an intricate nightmare, like the veins and arteries of a human body, and serves roughly the same function.

Aft again through yet another bulkhead into the oily, pulsing cavernous clamour of the engine room, where bare-knuckled pushrods hammer their persistent, raucous melody as they drive her two and a half thousand horsepower diesels that dominate each side of the metal footplate. Huge vibrating monsters that stretch from bilge to deckhead, and crowd in on me with their hot, oily bodies. Here men learn to lip-read, or pick up familiar orders without hearing the words. They know what may be allowed to heat up and what must be well-lubricated. They can recognise a new alien sound amidst all the din, and know when to be alarmed at what they hear. They live in this smelly world, starved of sunshine and fresh air, with the heavy stench of hot oil and diesel fuel seeping into their bodies for most of their lives, tending the living, breathing beast for days and weeks on end, while millions of counteracting forces snarl and bellow in their ears.

Beyond, a brighter, shiny cavern where gleaming arrays of levers and switches line up in copper ranks on switchboards and battery panels. An intricate assortment of controls and interlocks where nimble fingers flick and push to control the main electric motors when the engines are quiet and the clutches are out. They are oversized, sophisticated versions of car batteries that have to be kept at exactly the right temperature if they are to perform well and not explode in your face. They are subdued and less boisterous than their noisy neighbours, but they produce one thousand four hundred and fifty horsepower each, and are every bit as lethal if abused. One of the blessings of a dived boat is the soft whine of those two motors.

Right aft now, through the last bulkhead into the stokers' mess with its open toilet, and the steering gear. Above my head a third member of a trio of aft-facing torpedo tubes to give *Tarantula* a sting in her tail, all external, so that once fired they cannot be reloaded at sea.

That is a simple inventory. It would take volumes to describe in detail one part of her complicated workings. Suffice to say that amongst her company you will find someone who knows the function of every single instrument, switch and lever, and exactly what must be done in an emergency, or when things start to go wrong. Like us, sometimes she requires major surgery and has to be taken into dock, but mostly we can cope with her minor ailments.

Ultimate responsibility falls on the shoulders of one man. He is the maestro who must orchestrate the whole set-up. I sometimes wonder if we hold on to some of our experienced, successful skippers for too long. Men who have notched up victory after victory go back on patrol again and again, even though their nerves have become frayed and their senses dulled.

The Germans do it too. They have lost some of their best aces in the past year. Prien, Kretschmer, Schepke; all commanders who should have earned a spell ashore where they could be put to better use teaching others how to do the job. Would men like them not be well employed in command of escorts, with their knowledge of the tricks of the submarine trade? Some of ours look like ageing athletes who have hung on until they have burned themselves out. We know when to service the boats all right: do we know when a man is breaking down?

It is no use waiting for a captain to admit that the strain is telling either, or that he wakes up sweating beside an anxious wife when he is on leave. It is too much to expect these men to lose face and go to his captain S/M saying, 'I've had enough. I am beginning to get the shakes and cut corners, and I have a first lieutenant more capable than I at running the boat. If you don't relieve me I shall be responsible for the deaths of forty-odd other blokes.'

I shake away the thought. There are no problems like that with our skipper; just the opposite in fact. Some might say he is a bit too keen. His whole bearing exudes confidence, and he is every bit as fresh as he was on the day when I first met him when he took over command of his destroyer at Dunkirk after the captain was killed. I know him better than most, and I doubt if he even gives a thought to the tension that this awesome responsibility brings.

By the time I reach the control room most of the men have closed up for the special 'surface action stations' devised back in the Scottish lochs, and my place is on the bridge wheel. I climb up the tower without the familiar force ten gale tearing at my clothing, for we are on the electric motors now, allowing Trump to listen on his hydrophones for tell-tale noises. Even the ocean seems hushed as it stretches like black satin into the void. Once my eyes become fully adjusted I fancy I can see a faint lightening in the eastern sky as dawn begins to break. Beyond that distant rim the coast of Spain runs parallel to our course, and I know that coast well, for it verges the highway for all ships going south and east, and always seems to have a ridge of cumulus sitting over it, with the promise of warm sunshine just out of sight.

We are moving through the ocean like a knife through silk, with hardly a blemish on the glassy surface as Martingale holds the bow-wave down to a soft chuckle and our phosphorescent wake to minimum. Two lookouts, the signalman, the skipper and myself make up the bridge party in this special drill. Gunmetal shadows are taking substance as the light grows. The bridge telegraphs are unmanned, and all engine and motor orders are being passed down through the voicepipe to the man sitting below on the helmsman's seat. It is Martingale's idea to use the bridge helm in case we have to do some fancy manoeuvres.

Ten minutes ago Sparks picked up another series of 'V's, and the bearing seemed to confirm his earlier predictions. Now the navigator has drawn in an estimated target course and speed on his chart, though it is all guesswork to a degree, for as yet the radiomen have been unable to get an accurate fix. On a clear morning like this atmospherics play tricks with their equipment, and it is down to them to use their imagination to obtain a rough estimate.

The sky has become a lighter grey now and the circle of ocean is expanding, with folds of deep black in the long sweep of our bow-wave. Martingale concentrates with his night glasses on the sector where the telegraphists say we can expect to get our first glimpse of the enemy boat. Both lookouts are allocated arcs on either beam, while Bunts looks out astern. It is easy to imagine our counterparts on the bridge of that U–boat doing the same. Any second now she could blink a challenge with her hooded signal-lamp, half expecting one of her mates to respond with the correct code for the morning. With any luck she might hold back from reacting and curse the slack seamanship of this stranger if she believes we are responding to her summons like a good 'oppo' should.

'Object, red one five, sir!' reports the lookout in a hoarse whisper. 'It could be the bridge of a U–boat.'

'Very good!' Martingale makes a slight adjustment to his own glasses. The bearing is almost exactly where we would expect it to be. He responds to a call from the Asdic voicepipe, and I can just make out Trump's voice reporting. 'Fast HE off the port bow, sir. It could be a submarine's diesels.'

'Range?'

A moment's pause while the HSD checks his instruments, then, 'No definite range, sir, moving right to left. More than five thousand yards, I'd say.'

'I should bloody well hope so!' snorts Martingale derisively. 'Any closer and we could reach out and touch her. Listen carefully,' he tells us quietly. 'On a day like this we should hear her engines. Port five, coxswain!'

'Port five, sir – five degrees, port wheel on!'

'Steady!'

'Steady, sir – course one two five!'

'Steer one two zero!'

'One two zero, sir!'

'Look-out!' snaps Martingale with an edge to his voice.

'I've lost it, sir. I – I'm sure it was there though.'

'Very good.'

The dawn has a lifeless quality to it, and the sea is full of shadows. The false dawn quickly fades as we wait for the sun to rise. Every fold in the ocean could be a U-boat.

'Bearing now!' His tone is slightly tetchy, as though he is expecting more frequent reports.

Back comes Trump's unflustered voice. 'Almost dead ahead, sir. Still moving right to left. Estimated range now ten thousand yards – multiple HE in the background.'

'Good God!' exclaims Martingale caustically. 'That range has opened suddenly, hasn't it?'

'The signal is much clearer now, sir.' It is Trump's turn to show umbrage. 'There was a lot of quenching.'

'Very well!' He doesn't sound too pleased, but it is no use blaming Trump. There is a full assortment of strange noises playing havoc with his delicate instruments. Disturbance, differing densities, shoals of fish, other ships; even our own sounds, all combine to confuse him. If Trump says things are difficult, we can take that as read. The skipper's over-reaction shows how tensed up he is.

'Port ten – steer zero nine zero!'

Due east! I repeat the order and spin the wheel to bring her across the southerly breeze, with our bows pointing towards the dawn. That will give us a slim profile, while we should see her broadside on as she churns along on her diesels. At the moment we seem to be holding all the aces.

'Five bloody miles!' growls Martingale sourly. 'We'll lose her if we're not careful. Group up – full ahead together!' He scowls at us. 'Keep your eyes skinned – we should see her soon. Asdics!'

'Sir?'

'Have you a range on the convoy?'

This time Trump's reply is immediate. 'No sir. It is just a confusion of all types of HE. I would make a guess at about twenty thousand yards.'

That places the U-boat much closer to the convoy than originally estimated, and right between us. The escorts must know that she is there, and it puts our previous estimate out by about ten miles. The German is right where Martingale said he should be; a little ahead of the flank, and well within visual range. That is probably why she has not seen us. Her diesels will not allow the use of hydrophones, and they are concentrating on the convoy.

There is a thin yellow streak across the base of the cumulus now, and I can see Martingale's features etched with deep lines as he peers across the bow. The wind sings stealthily through the periscope standards and the ocean rolls gently with long, oily swells rocking *Tarantula* gently as she pushes along at about five knots. I shiver at a sudden chill as I think of how vulnerable we are. The skipper is breaking all the rules as we creep in naked towards the other boat. Right now several of her mates could be lining up for a shot at us. Our only defence is that they do not expect to see a British boat in their playground.

'Submarine – green three oh, sir!' The look-out's voice is tinged with excitement, even though he keeps it down.

'Very good!' Martingale concentrates hard. 'I've got her!'

I force my eyes to stay on the compass as a surge of trepidation runs through my veins like warm milk. Every report seems to belie the previous one, and the wind sighs mournfully as though it senses something going radically wrong. The metallic shapes of the bridge fixtures are taking form, with a tinge of red to them.

'Bridge!' The voice comes from the Asdic voicepipe. 'Fast HE approaching – green one five! Sounds like an escort!'

Martingale thumps the wooden capping on the bridge-rail. 'Blast! That puts her right in line with the target! We'll have to open up an angle or we will sink the escort along with the bloody U–boat. Starboard ten – in both engine clutches – full ahead together!' All caution thrown to the wind now as we swing into a tight turn.

'Blow up tubes one, two, three and four – look-outs below!' He bends over his sight, mouthing details into the voicepipe. 'Target is a U–boat – turning towards – range closing fast – approximately six thousand yards – estimated speed seven knots – I am thirty degrees on her port bow – control room steering!' He turns sharply. 'You can get below, Grant. Tell Number One to stand by for the fastest dive in history.'

'Tubes one, two, three and four flooded, sir,' comes the report just as I drop down through the hatch. When I reach the helm Guns is repeating, 'Open one, two, three and four bowcaps – what is my distance off track?'

The navigator comes back quietly with his estimate, and I can imagine Martingale lining up on the predicted spot where hopefully both torpedo and U–boat will meet. I ease the gunlayer out of his seat to take over the helm.

'Stand by!' Subby is beside me, feeding instructions into his torpedo-order panel, and the rating alongside him repeats the order over his mouthpiece as a double-check.

'Firing interval three seconds!' A tight spread. Tod Cooper will have his hand on the firing lever as he stares up at his repeater, where the responding lights flicker as Subby relays the orders from the control room.

'Fire!'

A distant thump, but no pressure on the ears as we would get if the boat was dived.

'All torpedoes running!' reports Trump.

The klaxon screams twice as the signalman's feet rattle on the ladder. The diesels choke to a stop and we hear the rush of air escaping from the ballast tanks. *Tarantula* is on her way down as I shift across to the after hydroplanes.

'Ninety feet!' The skipper is in the control room as the needle sweeps past twenty feet. 'I'm sure that she spotted us just as we fired,' he says grimly as he stares down at his stop-watch. 'Let's hope that we got it right this time.'

We all hear the explosion when it comes.

Five

For a moment there is no reaction from anyone. It is as though we can hardly credit our own ears, and it takes Trump's cold, methodical voice to confirm our hopes. 'Breaking up noises, sir. She is blowing air like mad – Christ!' He yells with agony and snatches his earphones away as we all hear the second explosion.

This time there is a cheer from some of the crew. 'That must have been her torpedoes going up,' says Martingale with quiet satisfaction. He looks about at our faces with a huge grin on his face. 'It looks like we have sunk our first U–boat, though I doubt if it is worth going up to search for souvenirs.'

He grabs the tannoy, and his steady voice quells the excited babble of chatter. 'Stand by to surface! We had better get up top fast, and establish our identity before the corvette begins to lob depth-charges at us.'

He swings round on the signalman. 'Follow me up closely with your Aldis. Make sure you have the challenge and response ready: I don't want any mistakes.'

'Aye aye, sir.'

The skipper takes one last look round. 'Right, let's go up fast. No time for a look through the periscope, we'll just have to take the chance.'

The ERA's fingers dart about the valve chest, feeding high pressure air into the tanks, and our hydroplanes go to 'full rise'. From ninety feet *Tarantula* planes up to broach like a big whale, spewing water from her drain holes. Before she has time to settle on an even keel Bunts will be flashing away at the corvette, before she recovers from her surprise and opens fire at us. The diesels burst into song and cool air is sucked down through the tower as we wait for the next orders to come from the bridge.

'Full ahead together – start the blowers – starboard fifteen!' The gunlayer repeats the order, and the telegraphs jangle as he spins the wheel. 'Fall out from diving stations – casing party up top with life lines to pick up survivors.'

'Survivors!' cries Falstaff incredibly. 'Who can have survived that lot?'

That is just what I am thinking as a cold hand clamps at my inside. And what is Martingale thinking about, stopping in mid-ocean when there must be other U–boats in the vicinity? In any case the corvette is much better equipped to pick up survivors than we are.

'First lieutenant to the bridge!' repeats the gunlayer in his expressionless tone. 'Stand by to receive casualties from the corvette.'

A sickening jolt hits my gut. I ease the gunlayer out of his seat and take over the helm. The word spreads like fire through the boat, and we no longer wish to look at each other.

'Coxswain!' Martingale's dead voice comes down the voice-pipe.

'Sir?'

'Put someone else on the wheel and gather as many blankets and as much warm clothing as you can find. Prepare bunks in the wardroom and messes. And warn Cooper that we may need to open the fore-hatch.'

'Aye aye, sir.'

I pass the helm over to someone and go bundling forward to find everyone standing about in a state of shock. Their faces turn towards me as I come through the bulkhead door. I drop my eyes for a second as I feel the accusation in their stares. It is grim in that stark grotto where they have just finished reloading numbers three and four tubes in record time. Tod is right up at the sharp end, his face pale and ghostlike in the yellow light. 'What the thundering hell have we done, Ben?' he asks.

'What do you mean?' I ask, avoiding his eyes.

'You know damned well what I mean. We have torpedoed one of our own ships.'

I square up to him. 'You don't know that for certain, Cooper. It's best to stow that kind of talk until we know the facts. Get your men rigging the tables and squaring up the stowage-space; we may have to use it as a sick-bay. Get as many blankets as you can find. Open up the hammocks and spread them on the tables and deck. Rake out as much spare clothing as there is too. It looks as though we are going to need all of it. While you are about it, rig a line onto the strong-back; we may have to open the hatch.'

I purposely keep the hardness in my voice, for I want to lift them out of the shock. There are simple bunks, no more than rectangles of metal piping with canvas stretched across, which can be attached to the torpedo-stowage clamps. Tod's men set to, shackling them into place and preparing the compartment in grim silence. The forehatch is angled into the boat to enable torpedoes to be lowered through, and there is a solid chunk of steel socketed into the short shaft to reinforce it. When the boat is dived the outside pressure clamps it tightly into place, making it immovable, and even on the surface it requires a line rove through an eyebolt in the deckhead to lift it out of its sockets. If we have to use the hatch I want it opened and shut in the shortest time possible, for it is almost at sea level.

Leaving them to organise things I go aft into the accommodation space, and run smack into Falstaff as he comes forward from the control room. His face is haggard and drawn in the artificial light, and when he sees me standing in his way it doesn't alter. 'We can use the wardroom for any serious cases, Grant. It is going to be up to us to do the best we can for anyone badly injured. Let's hope there is nothing too complicated. I take it you know how to administer morphine?'

My mind searches back to a course that I did long ago in Blockhouse, and I wish that I had taken a lot more interest. 'There are tablets in the medical chest, sir. A book of instruction too, I think.' I am ashamed to admit that I have not looked inside that chest since we commissioned, but I dimly recall syringes and phials amongst the contents when I signed for it. I have the feeling that when it comes to administering the stuff it will be either ineffective because I'm too cautious, or lethal because I can't stand screaming.

By the time the first walking wounded begin to filter down into the boat we have organised as much as we can to accommodate them. Most are in a semi-dazed condition, pathetically grateful as our lads usher them forward and ply them with hot soup and something stronger. Those who can, strip down and allow *Tarantula*'s men to remove their sodden garments as they stand in mute acceptance. All are wrapped in warm blankets and woollens.

A corvette's complement is about eighty-five, and it soon becomes obvious that only about a third have survived. So, although we are crowded, we manage to fit them all below with a bunk of some sort. That is quite an achievement, for I know of a U–boat that sailed back to base looking like a giant porcupine with her casing crowded with half-drowned seamen after she picked up the survivors of two of her own kind. We have four hundred or more miles to go, and even at full speed it will take us at least thirty hours through enemy-infested waters, with those big Kondors prowling about. It is good to know that we can dive in an emergency, even though Falstaff will have to wrestle with the problems of overweight.

Up to now the relatively healthy have arrived, and just when I am beginning to relax a little the order comes to open the fore-hatch. That is when the nightmare really begins. One by one the limp and writhing torsos are lowered down through the hatch and stretched out on the prepared hammocks or on bunks in the messes. Wide, staring, white-rimmed eyes glare out of blackened faces, glazed and half crazy as they plead with us to ease their agonies. Some are deadly quiet, with accusation written all over their features as the numbness begins to wear off with excruciating agony. Other gurgle and froth, with their gullets half-choked with oil and filth. Some retch and claw at our clothing with bony talons, half mad with fear and pain, while one man screams with monotonous intensity, and with one accord my so-called ship-mates pass him over to me.

I don't require a degree in medicine to see what is basically wrong with this bloke. His right leg is snapped below the knee, with a stark, white bone sticking out almost at right angles as it protrudes through the red, glutinous gash. I am on the point of running away and burying my head when Falstaff turns up with the medicine chest. 'Let's get him onto the table,' he says quietly. 'You look after the leg while I see what I can do this end. Now we shall see if this scream-quieter works.' He hovers over his patient for a second or so. 'God, friend; thou givest off a very ancient and fishlike smell!'

I leave him to his mumblings and try to shut my ears to the awful shrieks that come from the gaping mouth with the naked teeth. Someone is holding him down firmly as I take hold of the leg. I use my pusser's dirk to cut away loose boilersuit. The nausea loses its potency as I become immune to the sight of raw meat and the mixture of blood and gristle. Falstaff is going about his affairs with methodical precision as he studies instructions and measures out specified dosages. The patient continues to make a bloody nuisance of himself as he squirms and squeals.

'We are doing our best, you silly sod!' growls one heartless seaman beside me. 'It ain't our fault we're so bloody useless!'

Someone plunks a fat wad of cottonwool in my hand, along with a bottle of antiseptic. I stare down doubtfully and wonder what new crescendos the man will reach when I begin to go to town on his shattered leg.

Amazingly the shrieks die to a series of gurgling sounds. The limbs stop threshing about too as the leg goes slack in my hands. 'Hope I haven't given him too much,' remarks Falstaff as he replaces the gear.

The patient is lying back quietly now, even snoring in a queer, laboured sort of way. I take a deep breath and douse the wound, cringing for the expected explosion of reaction that should assail my ears. He doesn't even stir, and confidence begins to flow. 'Hold on while I try to straighten his leg,' I order Clump, whom I recognise as the one who is holding the patient down.

I take a firm hold on the foot with one hand, and the knee with the other. Adjust my stance like a golfer and offer up a silent prayer. The body jerks and there is a sharp hiss when I pull, but the bone doesn't budge. I straighten up and sigh. I am being far too cagey. It requires a sudden jerk – we've all seen Clark Gable do it. I brace up; take a firmer hold, hold my breath, and yank hard. It snaps back into the leg like magic, and I can hardly believe my luck. Steeling myself again, I delve into the wound to run my thumb along the bone, cautiously easing it into line until I can feel its smoothness matching up. This is the moment when he should go through the deckhead, but he remains slumped in sublime silence, without so much as a gurgle coming from his lips.

'I'll need something to lash it up,' I murmur gratefully.

'Don't bother,' mutters Falstaff dryly. 'He isn't going to need that leg anymore. I seem to remember reading somewhere that snoring is a sign of a headwound. I should have paid more attention to my end – sorry.'

I reel back into the passageway where other men are busy putting finishing touches to recumbent shapes that occupy the bunks and tables. There is plenty of gore and grime about, but mostly the wounds are gashes and cuts which require only elementary first aid. Though some lie perfectly still, too ill to respond, and too weak to complain. *Tarantula*'s men give all that they have, and no one mentions torpedoes as the boat picks up speed to head for Gibraltar.

It is a sombre T–boat that doubles up on her wires and ropes alongside the depot ship. Silently we open up the hatches and start to carry our gear inboard. Medical teams come down to take charge of the survivors, and some of the corvette's men who are healthy enough, take time to shake hands with our lads to show there are no hard feelings. There are others, however, who climb the long companionway with half-hidden condemnation written in their expressions. No one has struck up lasting friendships during the time we have looked after them. We try to put a brave face on it, but we get the impression that most of them are glad to see the back of *Tarantula* and her crew.

On one of my frequent forays through the boat to make sure she is being made shipshape again I run into Falstaff taking a long, pensive look at the chart-table. 'Was it one of our fish that got the corvette, sir?' I ask.

'That is always a possibility, Grant,' he says quietly. 'Though the torpedo would have to be at least ninety degrees off-track to hit her, and it is quite possible that the U–boat got a shot off from her stern tube just before we hit her. We may never know for certain. It would not be the first time a fish went haywire; some of the bloody things we use date back to the first world war.' He looks hard into my eyes. 'Of one thing you can be certain. We have nought to be ashamed about. The angle was right, and any torpedoes that missed the U–boat should have run clear.'

'I bloody well hope so, sir,' I say quietly. 'God, how I would like to believe that!'

We should be in excellent spirits, because our kit has arrived ahead of us and Gibraltar is overflowing with goodies that many of us have not seen since before the war. It is like Christmas at night, with no blackout, and the 'Rock' ablaze with shop windows filled with lavish displays, while Spanish music issues from the numerous places of entertainment. We should be able to wallow in it like a huge, sensuous bath; soaking away the long days and nights at sea, and restoring morale for our next patrol. No-one is in any mood to celebrate, however. We go out of our way to avoid the eyes of other submariners, for they are tarnished with the same stigma as the story gets about the escorts lying in the harbour. It might be over-reaction, but my back prickles when I enter the chiefs' mess in the depotship, and conversation dies.

Martingale disappears inboard soon after we tie up; carrying the control room log, the chart that was used during the attack, and various other documents pertaining to the episode with the U–boat and the corvette. Everyone knows where he has gone, and why he has been summoned. He will argue his case with senior officers, who will cast jaundiced eyes over the evidence, remember Boxwell's unfavourable reports, and draw their own conclusions.

For our part, we get queried by old acquaintances from other boats. Most of it is fairminded, and they take a sympathetic line, for they too have suffered from wayward torpedoes, and no one can actually rule out the possibility that the U–boat was responsible. It is when our lads get ashore amongst the men from the escorts that the booze begins to flow and the trouble starts.

By twenty-two hundred the first casualties begin to return with battle-scarred faces and hurt pride. It is not only our own men who suffer either, for we have created a rift between the general service lads and the submariners, and few stop to work out the facts when they hear about one of their own kind being put down. To some of those blokes off the escorts, submarines are tarred with the same brush; they are evil, stealthy back-stabbers who rip merchant ships apart and leave behind a stain in the sea like a running sore.

At tot time Tod comes to have a word with me in the depot ship's mess. He is concerned about Jennings who seems to blame himself for what happened. The PO Tel is a sad bloke to have about the place at the best of times, but since we arrived at Gib he has become even more morose, and he is giving everyone the shits. He mooches about the boat without speaking to anyone, and now he has not been seen for a couple of hours or more. His shore togs are still in his locker, so he must be somewhere in the depot ship.

It doesn't take me long to find him after a few enquiries, sitting like a bloody zombie in the ship's chapel. The padre is hovering about like an old crow, but Jennings is saying nothing to anyone. When I get there he is staring into space and looking more doom-laden than ever. The padre takes me to one side to tell me something ought to be done.

I can see his point. He doesn't want his chapel cluttered up with despondent PO telegraphists, but I don't see what I can do. 'What do you suggest, sir?' I ask sourly. After all, this is supposed to be his province: it is why we have padres; except for when some bloke has to be buried.

'Perhaps he should see a doctor.'

I look at his pale, almost transparent face. What can this bloke possibly know about submarines and what goes on inside them? 'He is not ill, sir,' I explain. 'He's just got his guts in a knot over what happened. There are two ways he can get it out of his system, and he chose this one; I thought you would have approved.'

'If that was the case, I would be only too happy to help, but he was downright rude when I tried to talk to him.'

'Maybe he don't want to talk.'

'But I am a padre!'

'Yes, sir.' Some sin-bos'n's I like – some I don't. This simpering bastard gives me the hump. His chapel looks like it is used once a year and polished every two hours. Jennings spoils the whole thing with his oily, aromatic submarine clobber. Some of the best blokes I know are padres, but there is this other kind too. 'He wouldn't have come here if he didn't need help, sir. What do you reckon I can say to him that you can't? With due respect, sir – you're the bloody sky-pilot!'

He jerks up angrily. 'I find your attitude offensive, chief. I will speak to your captain if you can't mind your tongue.'

'Sorry, sir. You've probably not heard about what happened.' I know damned well that he has – everybody has.

'That unfortunate business with the corvette, you mean?'

My eyebrows go up slightly. 'Yes, sir. That unfortunate business with the corvette. We are all feeling pretty lousy about it, and we all have our different ways of pulling out of it.' I look at Jenning's lonely shape sitting there, staring into space, and I sigh. 'I'll have a word with him.'

'There is one other thing,' he says secretly.

'Sir?'

'Are you C of E?'

'Yes, sir.'

'Well he isn't. He has rosary beads round his neck.'

'Good God!' I say in horror, and he darts a suspicious look at me. 'What I'm trying to say is that I can arrange for him to see a priest if he so wishes,' he explains irritably.

I am too dumbfounded to reply, and he looks at me as if I am some sort of idiot. 'Leave it to me, sir,' I assure him. 'I'll see what I can do to get rid of him.'

'Good!' he says, much relieved. 'You see, we have captain's rounds today, and the chapel has been cleaned.'

I watch him bustle off, and then go inside. The chapel is only the size of a large living-room, and all the more decorative and peaceful for that. Only the hushed breathing of the air-vents invades the sanctity, and I can see why Jennings chose this place to get away for a while. I sidle up and sit beside him. 'The padre reckons you're making his chapel look untidy.'

He remains as he is. 'It's the only place I could find to be on my own for a while. That stupid sod kept comin' to see if I was all right. I'm afraid I lost my temper in the end.'

I nod slowly. 'Want me to go away?'

'No.' He looks at me with his sad spaniel eyes. 'I was about to pack up and go anyway.'

'Want to talk about it?'

He looks down at his hands as they rest on his lap. 'If I had not been so bloody keen a lot of dead blokes would be alive now.' He holds a hand up to stop me interrupting. 'Don't tell me it wasn't my fault. I know that, but it don't make things any easier. It is the first time I've felt personally responsible for killin' anyone.'

We sit quietly for a few moments while I give him time to work it out. There is nothing I or anyone else can say; he's just got to jerk out of it himself. Eventually he rises and we go out onto the upper deck where the sun and noise hits us between the eyes. Far across the bay the coast of Spain is lined with small white houses that look like beachhuts, and the grey warships anchored between look entirely out of place.

'Some would say that you did a bloody good job, Sparks,' I tell him. 'There will always be cock-ups in war. Look how many times our boats get pounced on by friendly forces. It's almost become a joke.'

'Yeah, I know. I'll shake it off when we get to sea, I expect.' He slopes off despondently, leaving me alone with my own thoughts, which are not too far removed from his own.

I decide that I want a bit of time on my own too, but I am not the church-going type, so I find a remote spot on the seaward side of the mole where it slopes down into the warm, translucent water. The sun has warmed the stonework so that it seeps into my backside like a balm. I can sit alone with my thoughts and stare out across the blue ocean with my cap tilted forward to shade my eyes. In the distance the brown coastline of North Africa stretches away to the east, and I fancy I can smell the burnt tang of the desert. The war seems a long way off.

Who can imagine anything as loathsome as a submarine sneaking along beneath such a benign sea? It looks so innocuous as it stretches like a glass sheet towards the east, as though it has never heard of exploding ships, bloated corpses, or men who die with bones sticking out of their legs. I lie back and push my cap even further forward to cut out the sun, relishing a soft breeze from the sea.

'Swain!'

The sound of Clump's falsetto voice makes me wince as it penetrates the peace from the other side of the ridge. I am tempted to lie back and ignore him, but I know that someone must have seen me come this way, and that he will seek me out to the end. Reluctantly, with a great deal of stretching, I straighten up and push my cap back into place before climbing slowly over the top.

His voice has become a monotonous chant as he plods along past the looming bulks of capital ships moored alongside. This is home for the mighty Force H, consisting of a couple of battle-wagons and a battle-cruiser, along with an aircraft-carrier, cruisers and about twenty destroyers. Add them to a host of other ships that come in from the Atlantic and you get a very busy harbour. It must keep Nazi spies well occupied on the Spanish mainland as they monitor comings and goings.

We are having a sticky time as 1941 draws to a close. The Germans and Italians are bombing hell out of Malta. The *Ark Royal* has been sunk, and the poor old *Barham* blew herself to blazes as she rolled over after being torpedoed. The enemy seems to be having things all his own way, with the whole Itie navy concentrating its ships in the enclosed area of the Central Mediterranean. It's their playground all right, with air-cover from hundreds of bases where it matters most. Any ship trying to run the Malta blockade must take on that lot, plus the huge minefields in the narrows and round the island itself.

I shake these grim thoughts away when I realise that Clump is attracting attention from the lofty quarterdecks. It is not every day they see a lanky, scruffy, torpedoman in outsized boots ambling along the jetty shouting, 'Swain!' at regular intervals. There are ten blokes for every job in those monsters, and they have plenty of time to stand and stare.

'Perry!' I yell, snapping every eyeball in my direction.

He swivels under the gaze of a hundred men, and his face lights up in recognition. 'Swain!' he repeats joyously as he trips over a mooring rope. 'The skipper wants yer!' He picks himself up and shambles towards me with his face split into a huge grin. I am conscious of officers staring down at our antics from the imperious quarterdecks. They belong to another navy; remote from the submarine world. Even in wartime the elaborate trappings of traditional pomp is there. The brightwork might be painted over and the sides camouflaged, but there are telescopes on those quarterdecks and haughty faces peering down from beneath brass-bound cap-peaks. It is a totally alien world to the likes of Clump and me, and it always makes me feel extremely uncomfortable. The torpedoman doesn't help either, for he typifies the big-ship perception of the submariner as a slightly insane, inebriated reprobate with an aversion to good order and discipline.

I would like to march smartly away with him, but Clump has not learned to walk with any dignity, let alone march. His oily boots splay like duck's feet and he has the exaggerated roll of a drunken ploughman. 'What's the problem?' I ask, trying to take my mind away from the embarrassing stares.

'Dunno, Swain. The skipper wants ter see yer in 'is caboosh; that's orl I know.'

'Just me?'

'Far as I know.'

Curiosity makes me increase pace, leaving him to shuffle along behind as best he can. I find Martingale trying to adjust the big windscoop in his open scuttle to funnel in the breeze. I tap on the open door and step across the sill without waiting for an invitation.

'The first lieutenant says that all is ready for sea, Grant. Does that apply to your department?'

That's a strange question. He knows full well that Falstaff would never make that report without checking with me first. 'Yes, sir. My stores are on board, and we have a healthy company.'

'Have we?' He swings to face me. 'Jennings has reported sick.'

'He must have done so after I left the boat this morning, sir.'

'The problem is that the depot ship's doctors can find nothing wrong with him. He complains of stomach cramps, pain and nausea. Could it be psychological?'

My mind leaps back to the chapel and Jennings's mournful countenance. He has all the right symptoms perhaps, but that goes for most of us. 'He did a damn good job with the huff duff on that U–boat, sir. Led us straight to her: him and Trump.'

'That's just it: Maybe he has a warped sense of guilt about the outcome. He is a very introverted character. Do you think that he could be losing this nerve?'

I shrug my shoulders. 'Only a head-shrinker can tell us that for sure, sir.'

'I haven't got time for that. There is something big coming up, and *Tarantula* is involved. Jennings is a good telegraphist;

too good to leave inboard without good reason. We all get our guts in a knot at times, and what sort of replacement would we get at such short notice? The last thing I want is to break up the team now that we have it working so well, and he has proved his worth in the WT office. The snag with men like him is that he has no close mates to tell if there is anything wrong at home.'

'That's true enough, sir. I have already spoken with him, and although he feels badly about what happened, I don't think he's malingering.'

'Well, have another go at him. I know it's a difficult job, but we have only twenty-four hours to make a decision. You can tell him that it is in his own interest too, for if we do leave him behind and the doctors confirm that there is nothing medically wrong with him he could face a charge of desertion, and he is too good a man for that. Lay it on hard and let me know how he reacts, and what you think.'

He changes tack. 'There's another problem. I know that there has been a lot of wild talk about what happened with that corvette, and our lads have run into bother on shore. I want you to tell everyone that experts have gone over the details of our approach and attack with a fine-toothed comb and are satisfied beyond doubt that there must have been a fault in the guiding system of the torpedo. Therefore, no blame is attached to *Tarantula*, and there is nothing for which we have to feel guilt.'

'They will be glad to hear that, sir. Most of them are feeling pretty lousy about what happened.'

He darts a suspicious look at me, as though he detects a hidden meaning behind my words, then changes the subject. 'We are loading cargo for Malta and there will be no shore-leave tonight. Mail will close at sixteen hundred so that we can complete censoring, and I want every man on board the boat by eighteen hundred. There is no way that we can keep our destination secret. Anyone with half an eye can see the nature of the goods we are carrying, but that does not mean that we have to go about broadcasting it. Understood?'

'Right, sir.'

He relaxes and smiles at me. 'One personal note, Grant. You will be glad to learn that Laura has not been sent to the Tower for giving away trade secrets. She is still with Captain Boxwell, and I happen to know that he and his staff are being flown out to Alex. So there is every chance of seeing her again.' He looks at my blank expression and his smile fades. 'Well, I thought that you might be interested.'

'Thank you, sir.' Course I'm bloody interested! It is his attitude that I cannot understand. It is as though he sees Laura as some pet that we are both sharing.

I go down to the casing where a chain of sweating matelots are passing an assortment of boxes and crates down through the hatch. The weight, and the way the contents are packed shows that there are intricate pieces of machinery amongst it. Small, expensive items that make up a vital cargo; important enough to warrant a special trip. I know that there is a shortage of replacement items for submarine in Malta, and by the sound of it things are not going to improve.

It is mid-afternoon before I manage to get Jennings on his own again. We stand at the rail of the depot ship, looking out across the harbour while all the activity of a boat preparing for sea goes on below us. I feel guilty about being up here when my place is in the boat, checking and stowing my supplies, but this is the last chance I'll get, for by the way fuel and stores are coming on board that twenty-four hour time limit that Martingale spoke about is shrinking all the time.

'How's the stomach?' I ask by way of an opener.

He grunts. 'Much the same. I have not eaten a thing since yesterday, and I keep getting a pain right here.' He points a thumb at his midrift. 'I know it isn't just a normal guts-ache, or a touch of foreign stomach trouble that the quacks talk about, but it is no use trying to argue with that lot; they think everyone is trying to pull a fast one.'

I haven't time to mess about. 'You are not still worrying about what happened with the corvette, are you? Some blokes get guts-ache through nerves, and not even know the cause. You'll never live it down if the doctors put you down as a malingerer.'

He swings on me. 'Think that, do you? I don't feel any guilt about that corvette; just a big sadness. I did what I was paid for, and it was Martingale who pulled the trigger. If I say I've got a bad stomach, that's what I've got.'

'Okay, okay,' I say, trying to take the heat out. 'Did they give you any medication?'

'If you can call bicarbonate of soda medication.'

'Right. Well, we shall be in Malta in a week's time. You should be able to hold on until then, surely?'

His features suddenly go deadly serious. 'I'm bloody scared, Ben. Scared of what is going on inside me. I know that there is something seriously wrong. You know as well as I do that there is no guarantee that we will reach Malta in seven days. We could be at sea three weeks and more. Once we leave harbour there is no coming back, or nice, cosy, friendly destroyer handy with a doctor on board, just waiting for me to be transferred over by jackstay. Once I am battened down in that cigar-shaped bastard, there I stay until we get back into harbour. It is my word against the quack's, and I think he has malingering on the bloody brain.'

I am half believing him now. Even if there is nothing physically wrong he is no state to go to sea, yet unless he is genuinely ill they will treat him like a criminal. 'You know the drill, Sparks. If the doctor says you are fit for duty, there it stands. You are our best radioman, and the skipper is not going to lose you if he can. If some blokes acted the way you are we would be glad to see the back of them, but it is different in your case. Try and stick it out to Malta. I'll make sure you are given all the rest possible.'

He slumps in despair. 'You mean that I have made myself indispensable, Ben. If I was lousy at my job I would be allowed to plead sick. I have never met a duff PO Tel in submarines, so Martingale could get a replacement if he had a mind to. What really gets to me is that no one, not even you, believes me.'

I say nothing. Deep down I know that what he is saying is true. Our bunting tossers and sparkers are amongst the best in the world, and although Jennings ranks amongst the best of those, he is by no means indispensable, and the chances are that any replacement will be just as efficient. But the doctors have proclaimed him fit and Martingale wants to keep him in the boat, so he hasn't got a cat's chance in hell of getting relieved. Nevertheless I decide to have one more go for him. 'I'll have a word with Falstaff, and see what he has to say.' I pat his shoulder. 'If it means anything, Sparks; I don't think you are putting it on.'

He bangs his hand down hard on the rail. 'Sod the fucking

Andrew, and all the poxy doctors. Even if what I've got is brought on by a blue funk, it is still an illness, for Christ's sake!'

I struggle with my thoughts for a moment, then straighten up to move away. 'It's too bloody complicated for me, mate. I will do my best, that's all I can promise.' I leave him staring after me with that old, familiar hang-dog expression. If he has gone sour, he is only one out of sixty, and that isn't a bad average. Tomorrow we are all going to experience a tremor or two in our bellies when we slide out to sea, shut the hatches, and settle down for another spell in the hostile arena that everyone calls the 'Sunny Mediterranean'.

I will say this for Falstaff. He listens to what I have to tell him and takes it seriously enough to go and have a few words with the doctor, but when he returns the diagnosis is unchanged. As far as the medics are concerned Sparks is a healthy man.

We single up early next morning and slide out through the sunlit sea astern of the escort with Jennings still in the boat. If anything I would say he is looking much better now that the decision has been taken, and because he is such an introverted bloke no one bothers to find out if he is improving or not as we take our first trim dive to allow Falstaff to find out whether he has his sums right after allowing for all the extra weight we have taken on. The Med is an unfriendly place for submarines, for its transparency makes it possible for airmen to spot a lean shape even when it is dived. Each time we come up for air the odds are that there will be a reception committee waiting for us, and in the time it takes for Martingale to take a good look round, some lurking bomber could drop its load right where it hurts most. So it is more than just the semi-tropical heat that makes us sweat.

On the first day out he puts us in the picture. He has done a lot of talking over the tannoy lately, and I know it is not his favourite occupation, but he likes to keep his crew well informed about what is going on. He explains how different the situation is out here, compared to the Atlantic. Britain is hungry for millions of tons of dry cargo and oil to survive, while out here each individual ship that fights its way through to Malta can have a profound effect on the island's resources. In place of the big convoys of fifty or sixty merchantmen, with their escorts of destroyers and corvettes, whole battle-fleets are used to guard as little as six merchantmen. Front line warships with massive fire-power that will see a single battered ship through until she arrives in Grand Harbour, where she is greeted as a celebrity. The ramparts of Valletta are lined with cheering, relieved people when such a ship gets through.

With the *Ark Royal* gone, and *Illustrious* so badly damaged she must go the USA for repairs, we are short of air-cover. The Luftwaffe has brought its crack anti-ship Fliegerkorps X to back up the Italian Regia Aeronautica in a concerted effort to starve and terrify the Maltese people and garrison into submission, and it looks as though it is coming to a climax as we get closer to Christmas. Each squaddy should receive four thousand calories a day on active duty; the blokes in Malta are lucky to get half that, and there are 'Victory Kitchens' dishing out goat stew to the locals.

As we settle to our first meal one of the telegraphists comes racing forward to the wardroom with the news that the Japanese have bombed Pearl Harbour. 'The Yanks are in the war now, sir,' he says excitedly.

'The wheel is come full circle,' quotes Falstaff.

'It is nice to have the Americans on our side,' muses Martingale thoughtfully. 'There is only one snag.'

'What's that, sir?' asks Subby.

'We've got the whole Jap nation to fight as well as the Germans and the Italians.'

Six

'What do you think it is?' The query comes from Martingale when he comes blustering on to the bridge after being rudely awakened at two a.m. by myself and Subby as we share the middle watch. We are into a routine now; splitting the bridge watches between the three officers and myself, so that the skipper is spared from standing any watches at all. It is our first night out from Gibraltar and we have made good progress despite zig-zagging throughout the daylight hours.

There is a new accessory on the bridge in the form of a pack of old playing cards which we use as a timer and indicator. Someone will cut the pack, and if he turns up a black five we go five degrees to starboard for five minutes, add a nought, then go back on to our mean course for fifty minutes. If it turns out to be red queen we go twelve degrees to port for twelve minutes, then back on course for one hundred and twenty, and so it goes. It causes almost as much confusion to ourselves as to a potential enemy, for no one can anticipate when the next zig or zag will occur, and at one time it looked as though we might end up in the middle of the Sahara Desert following a succession of black cards. Eventually, however, it righted itself, and by midnight on the first day we are more than one hundred and fifty miles from where we started.

Since dropping our escorting destroyer we have not seen another vessel of any kind. We know that many of our ships are busily employed ferrying troops into Tobruk now that the siege has been lifted, but our own bland horizon remains remarkably unblemished hour after hour, and the sky perfectly speckless.

From tomorrow morning we go into a new routine whereby we dive all day and come up to breathe and recharge batteries at night. It will slow us up a lot, but we are entering a very hostile zone. By mutual consent I serve the rum after we surface at dusk, and we have our big meal of the day. I split the first and second dog watches with Subby, and we stand the middle watch together. So far there have been no alarms at all.

Now the incoming wind has brought a stink foul enough to turn my stomach. Martingale is none too pleased at being routed out of his bunk for a stink, but he would never have forgiven us if we had not called him. He has blinked himself into full consciousness and is testing the air with the rest of us, so that we resemble three stray mongrels catching the scent of a bitch on heat.

'God!' he chokes. 'What a bloody pong! What the hell can produce a stench like that?'

'Maybe we should just ignore it and go away,' suggests Subby hopefully. 'It could be quite unhealthy.'

'Not a chance! Much as I hate to say it, I think this bears investigating.' He bends to the voicepipe and mouths the orders that knock off the diesels and puts us on the quieter electric motors, at half speed.

It is a fairly lively sea, bucketing in from the starboard quarter with hundreds of small greybacks scuffed up by a blustery wind. *Tarantula* is in one of her lively moods, making life difficult for the helmsman and setting all the crockery a-jingle in the messes. One moment she is poised with her arse in the air, and the next she is scooping up froth with her bulbous bows as the swells slide under her belly. It is an untidy rhythm that no one can get used to, and there is the odd curse as she catches someone off-balance. Slowing down to two fifty revolutions to plod along at about seven knots doesn't help to make her stable.

'I don't think I want to see this,' declares Subby ruefully.

We have come round to starboard, bringing the stink right across the bow, and with every gust it becomes more pungent. 'Keep your eyes peeled,' warn Martingale.

'Mine are peeled and watered,' moans Subby.

'Shut up and concentrate!'

Martingale has hardly stopped speaking when I notice something looming out of the murk. All eye follow my outstretched arm as I report it. A grey smudge is wallowing half-submerged just beyond the bow as we slow to three knots and creep in on it. Suddenly everyone is whispering, and there are more shapes pass down each side.

'It's a bloody donkey!' exclaims a look-out. 'Look at 'im! Blowed up like a barrage balloon, wiv 'is legs in the air!'

Sure enough, a whole armada of bloated equine corpses move by in slow, undulating procession, but the main source of the stink comes from a solid mass of wreckage taking shape in the murk beyond its ghoulish outriders. As we draw nearer it looks like one of those trim schooners that ply the Mediterranean with all manner of cargoes, legal and otherwise. It is lying on its beam-ends, completely awash, with an unwholesome mess spewing out of the hold with every roll.

We are running up to windward now, thank God. The wind becomes easier on the nostrils, and as we get even closer we can see that she has been damaged by gunfire. Whoever started the job must have been interrupted before he could finish it, by the look of things.

'We should take a closer look,' states Martingale with no real enthusiasm. 'There could be something amongst that mess that could prove of value to our intelligence boys. They seem particularly adept at making something out of nothing. Who knows, we might find a crate of booze labelled "Kesselring".'

'That's not all we might find,' snorts Subby with a shudder. 'If you could bottle that and drop it on Germany we could win the war inside a week.'

'I won't tell you again to shut up, Sub.' Martingale bends to the Asdic voicepipe. 'Make a careful sweep round and report anything you hear.'

We all wait in silence while Trump's lad trains his aerial and calls back to say that he can hear nothing except breaking up noises close to on the starboard beam, and we all know what that is.

Martingale makes up his mind. 'All right, we'll take a close look.' Once more he calls down to the control room, this time using the helmsman's voicepipe. 'Diving stations – ask the first lieutenant to come up top – port ten!'

Tarantula makes a slow circle away from the offensive hulk, and Falstaff arrives just as the bows are coming back in line with the floating garbage. He wrinkles his nostrils. 'Gad! It appears no other thing to me but a foul and pestilent congregation of vapors!'

'Since you like it so much you had better go and take a good look,' says Martingale bluntly.

'I do begin to have bloody thoughts.'

'Well keep them to yourself and get on with it. I will push the bow right up to it. So set aside your aversions and go forward with the second coxswain and a willing heart.'

Falstaff sniffs. 'This is well beyond the call of duty.' However, he climbs over the bridge side with Jumbo and goes forward along the casing as Martingale eases *Tarantula* towards the wreckage at snail's pace until the bow nudges into a section of splintered timber that was once the poopdeck. In spite of the gloom both boarders manage to scramble across without mishap, and after casting disdainful looks at the mess that surrounds them they catch their breath and balance to climb down into a waterlogged wheelhouse.

Apart from the stench there are some weird sounds coming from the wreck as the timbers work against each other in the swell. The black ocean undulates mysteriously into infinity on either side, and stars blink innocently at our nocturnal activity. Our ears and eyes are tuned for the slightest suspicious noise or shadow, and we place our trust in the Asdic boys as we wallow with the nose pressed into the wreckage; providing a sitting target for any would-be assassin who happens along, and can get into a firing position.

We get away with it, however. Everyone sighs with relief when Falstaff and Jumbo leap back onto the bow and make their way aft along the slippery steel deck. Martingale is eager to get away, and the motors are going full astern before the two men reach the bridge, handing several items up to the lookouts before coming over the side themselves. The diesels thunder into life again and everyone breathes easier.

'The crew must have abandoned her in a hurry,' explains Falstaff, 'because we found a half-eaten meal scattered about the place, and they left behind all their worldly goods before taking off. All the stink is coming from the hold where a whole range of perishables are rapidly deteriorating into a putrid mess. We scratched about the flooded interior and found little of any consequence, except for these.' He holds up a black leather attaché case and a selection of sodden stationery. 'Looks Italian to me.'

Martingale takes it and turns it over in his hands. 'It's been ripped about a bit. There's part of it missing, where the lock should be.'

'That's what made me look again. When I shone my torch on it I could see an inscription in Italian and it looked very expensive. I guess the crew fished it out of the drink a few days before they were attacked, so we set about searching more thoroughly and found some papers and a small, hide-bound diary. The inscription reads "Decima Flottiglia Mas", and I happen to know that it means "Tenth Light Flotilla". They are the specialist boys who use explosive boats – EMBs they call them – and midget submarines. The Itie army might lack a bit of zeal, but, believe me, this lot are second to none when it comes to guts and determination.'

'Absolutely!' agrees Martingale tersely. 'I think you might have something here. They had a go at Malta back in July. It was a brave effort, but except for the damage they did to the viaduct in the breakwater they didn't achieve much. Not surprising; it was a suicidal enterprise against the island's defences.'

'Their whole set-up is suicidal if you ask me. Take those EMBs for instance. They are manned by blokes sitting on ejector-seats, and the idea is to be thrown clear just before they hit their targets.'

'Jesus!' I blurt out involuntarily.

'Exactly, Cox'n. They are "not in the role of common men" as the Bard would say. However, although the loose documents are well nigh illegible, the diary had a brass clasp holding it tightly shut, and the crew didn't bother to open it. There are several mentions of the word *maiale* which is the word the enemy uses for their two-man torpedoes. The attaché-case was empty and badly slashed, as you can see. It is fairly obvious that it was fished out of the drink, and as these torpedoes are carried in containers on the casing of submarines, I think we can draw our own conclusions.'

'Take it below,' orders Martingale. 'It will take those wizards of intrigue in intelligence to work out this lot. We'll deliver it to the underground op's room beneath the Lascaris bastion in Malta. They'll know what to do with it.'

After the boarding party and all spare bodies have cleared the bridge, Martingale settles the boat on course for the Skerki Channel, then goes below himself. I glance at my watch to find that the whole episode has taken no longer than forty minutes, and there remains an hour or so of my watch to complete before I too can slide down below, into my bunk. I resume my duties with a feeling of anti-climax and a complete lack of enthusiasm. Both Subby and I are more than glad to hear Falstaff blustering up to relieve us at eight bells.

Down below the boat seethes with the stagnant odour of sleeping men. I peel off my oilskins and prepare to turn in. No one undresses at sea, so I clasp the edge of my bunk to hoist myself in, then freeze when I realise that I have lost any inclination to sleep. Not wishing to disturb my messmates I go aft again into the control room where I find Jumbo sitting disconsolately on the after hydroplane seat. His blunt, bearded face is set in a mournful expression and his heavy shoulders are slumped wearily as he stares down at the cortecine deck. Like most, I tend to avoid the big second coxswain, for although he does his job well enough, and his vast strength makes him prime candidate for any special job that comes along, he is a bit of a maverick with his bitter, foul-mouthed abrasive humour. He can demolish a young seaman just by looking at him.

Right now he sits with his legs sprawled across the deck, staring into space, and totally ignored by the other men in his watch, who are taking their turns at the helm or on lookout. If he mends his ways he could soon be promoted and become coxswain of his own boat, but he will have to curb his tongue, and become far more amenable before anyone will consider him ready for it. Because there is nothing else to do I decide to have a word with him.

'What are you looking so bloody cheerful about?' I chaff lightly.

'Dunno,' he says without looking up. 'It's all those donkeys I suppose. Poor bastards; they ain't 'ad nuffin ter do wiv the fuckin' war. It's us stupid sods who seem ter like going about shootin' the hell out of each other; not them. What a soddin' mess we make of everythin'!'

'We don't make the decisions, for Christ's sake!'

'Oh, and that makes yer feel better, does it?' he snarls, lifting his eyes to glare at me. 'There's everybody feelin' sorry fer the blokes orf the corvette 'cause they're the same as ourselves. Puts us on a 'igher level than stinkin' donkeys, p'raps. Eases the conscience ter say 'ow sorry we are after we've knocked off 'alf a ship's company. Well, it is a load of bollocks, Swain. We get all we deserve, and there is too many words wasted on all that sentimental bilge.'

'I see,' I comment drily.

'No yer don't. You're no different ter orl the rest of the hypocritical bastards, and what makes me sick is that I found myself joinin' the club before I saw them donkeys. It's all a bloody farce, mate. Feelin' sorry for someone don't make us anything less than a lot of trained killers.'

I glance at the helmsman and his mates. They are studiously ignoring us, but you can almost hear their minds working. 'Everyone's entitled to his beliefs, Jumbo. I have never known you treat blokes badly, even though you scare the living daylights out of them. No matter how green and useless they are, you still find time to show them the way things are done, so you can't hate all the human race. If you was to stop trying to be the hardnosed second cox'n you might find us easier to live with.'

'Piss orf!'

I stand and glare down at him. 'I'll pretend that I haven't heard that, but don't push it too far, Moore, or you'll be lifting your lid in front of the skipper. You will treat me with respect, and don't you forget it.'

He doesn't answer so I leave him sitting in isolation while I go forward to try my bunk again. Even though I don't sleep it is pleasant to lie on my back with my head close to the hull and listen to the sea singing past only an inch or so away. It has taken a cargo of stinking donkeys to give me an insight into the strange workings of Jumbo's mind, and now I think I know what makes him such a hostile bastard. Usually when an NCO acts the way he does in submarines it is not long before he gets a one way ticket back to General Service, where he'll do less harm. They have more space than us for odd-balls, and even seem to favour loud-mouthed, belligerent POs with hard voices and soft brains. However, there is something in Jumbo's make-up that makes him fit into boats. For one thing, he is a good man to have about in a crisis, and he seems completely unemotional, despite all that bilge about donkeys. On many occasions his vast strength has helped the casing party out of a jam, and on balance, I reckon we would be a lot worse off without him.

An hour before sunrise we go to diving stations as Martingale prepares to take a final look round before he takes *Tarantula* down below for the day. She rolls broadside on for a while before the tannoy shrieks and the vents thump open, then we glide down into the Cimmerian depths to hide amongst tenebrous undercurrents, away from the sun and the wind, swimming through a world of translucent, wraithlike shadows, with only the soft whine of the electric motors and the occasional suck of hydraulics to serenade our souls. It is utterly peaceful, and if we really try we can shut our minds to the fact that each passing hour brings us seven miles closer to a huge minefield that some say stretches for over one hundred miles.

So far we have made excellent progress, and the long dusty coastline of Africa between Oran and Algiers slides by just below the starboard horizon. Now it will become much slower as we follow strict orders to remain dived all through the day, and avoid other ships like the plague; except for capital targets. Our precious cargo supersedes all other considerations as we press on towards Malta. The three hundred and fifty miles we have already under our belt is a bonus. All we can hope for from now on is about two hundred and fifty miles every twenty-four hours, and in two days we will enter the narrows between Sicily and Cape Bon where those huge minefields are waiting.

The Regia Aeronautica and the Luftwaffe will be patrolling the area; for their friends in Algeciras and La Linea will have told them we are coming, and they will have worked out our ETA. The Fliegerkorps X consists of some of the best pilots in the world, and have earned grudging respect from the men of ships like the *Illustrious* when their Stukas came screaming out of the sky from twelve thousand feet, split into two groups so that one lot could hold the attention of the two accompanying battleships, while the main force hurtled down in near perpendicular dives to blast hell out of the carrier. There are those who swear that some of the 'planes pulled out so late they flew along the flightdeck below the height of the funnel. *Tarantula* would offer a prime target to those boys if they spot her lean body sliding through the clear water.

As if that is not enough, Malta has her own crop of mines sown all round her with the dedicated precision of a farmer looking for a good yield. Convoys have to be led through by an advanced guard of minesweepers, and at one stage they even used depth charges to blast a clear channel. All we can hope is that the channel has not been re-sealed overnight by Italian floatplanes and E–boats who seem extremely adept at shutting the gap; and who can say where the odd stray mine has been missed to bob about in eager anticipation of opening up our bows like a peeled banana?

We are getting deeper into the enemy's background. He is on the sidelines watching and listening for us, and we have still a long way to travel, both in miles and sweat, before we berth alongside the wooden pontoons that reach out from the stone-flagged jetties of Manoel Island, and the submarine base of HMS *Talbot*. Under these circumstances even Martingale must conform and follow guidelines set out by those who govern the complicated defences of the beleaguered island. Our own forces will know approximately where we are, and if we pop up somewhere different we deserve all we get, and our own blokes will be on to us like a swarm of hornets.

At noon Tod Cooper comes to tell me that Sparks has taken to his bunk after collapsing in the WT office. He is doubled up with pain and nursing his stomach while he coughs up a mixture of bile and dark blood.

'Tell Falstaff and the skipper,' I tell him. 'I'll go and take a look at him.'

I slide out of the mess and go next door to the POs' mess where Jennings is rolling in agony and muttering strange things between bouts of coughing and groaning. Someone has produced what once was a white towel, but is now stained and damp as he chokes into it. He writhes about, drenched in sweat, and his skin is the colour and texture of old parchment. I wipe away some of the sweat and put my face close to his. 'Try to lie still, Sparks.'

He rolls his eyes towards me and stops thrashing for a couple of seconds. He looks ghastly, with pain-filled eyes that peer up at me with a pleading, glassy stare. There is mucus and slime on the stubble of his chin and his lips are trembling as they bubble with a frothy, red-tinted mixture. I look at the colour of the blood and know enough to realise that the dark, almost maroon shade means that it is coming from deep down inside his digestive system. He is sucking air with a sort of hissing noise as he goes into another bout of convulsions, while I just stare down at him helplessly.

'How is he?' asks Falstaff when he comes to peer over my shoulder, and I back off gratefully; relieved to have someone else take the weight for a while. Jennings's eyes flicker from one helpless face to another, searching for succour from his inadequate shipmates. It is a look that we would all like to run away from; a pleading, angry look that condemns us all for being so bloody helpless.

'I – I'm burning up!' he says in one of his more lucid moments. 'My guts is on fire. For Christ's sake give me something to ease the pain!'

He groans and wretches again. Rolling into his sodden towel while the whole accommodation compartment becomes hushed as the sound of his suffering stills the voices and takes their minds away from the letters they are writing and the books they are reading. We live in a world of healthy young men, where sickness is alien and intrudes into our lives like an unwelcome stranger when it comes. The blood and guts of battle is tolerated, for it is part of the game, but it is hard to come to terms with disease and illness. With every groan Sparks becomes more of a bloody nuisance to those who try to close their ears to his noise.

'I reckon I know what's wrong with him,' states Tod from the background. 'My old man had the same symptoms as these.' He nudges my arm and nods his head towards the wardroom, so I slide out with Falstaff, leaving a couple of POs to watch over the patient.

He keeps his voice down to a thick whisper. 'I am almost certain that it is a burst stomach or duodenal ulcer. It is following the same pattern as my dad. He had been complaining of feeling grotty from time to time with long periods of being okay before he got really sick; just like Sparks. If you add that to the bad air and lousy food it is hardly surprising that he comes up with something like this. He's a worry-guts too, just like my old man, and that gnaws at a man's guts, churning up the gastric joices so that they get to work on the lining of the stomach until an ulcer forms, and if it ain't seen to it burns a hole right through the lining. It allows the acidy mixture to leak into the whole of the insides. It's like having a burst appendix – peritonitis, they call it.'

'Well, what do we do about it?' asks Falstaff.

Tod sighs heavily and lowers his voice even more. 'They bundled my old man into an ambulance and broke all the speed limits and crashed every set of traffic lights to get him to hospital. He was stretched out on the operating table within an hour of the quack deciding that he needed his insides cleaned out, and he still died. I doubt that there is anything we can do except make him as comfortable as possible. Up to the time when the ulcer bursts you've got a chance if you feed him with bicarbonate, or even milk to dilute the acid, but once it gets to this stage he's had it.'

'How do you know it is perforated?' I ask.

He looks at me with solemn eyes. 'Just look at that mess and the way he is coughing up blood. The way he is writhing about I wouldn't give him more than twenty-four hours; you don't have to be a doctor to see how bad he is.'

'It's a pity the doctors didn't believe him,' declares Falstaff angrily. As though in agreement Sparks emits a long, soulful groan that reaches right down to my boots.

'We've got to do something for the poor bastard,' I plead.

'What do you suggest?' snaps Falstaff testily. 'It is quite obvious that we cannot put anything into his stomach. If this was a nice, cosy hospital someone could come along, look down with professional wisdom and proclaim him terminally ill, then administer drugs that would enable him to die in peace. If I pump morphine into him I could be killing him or turning him into a drug addict for no good reason. I think I'll go and have a word with the captain.'

Martingale is aft in the motor-room discussing the charging arrangements with the electricians, and when Falstaff brings him forward his face is sick with concern. We leave them standing together over the patient, who has suddenly gone mercifully quiet as he lapses into a semi-coma.

Tod places a hand on my sleeve. 'Why bother to ask Martingale? If it had not been for him Sparks would be in hospital now, receiving the right treatment. He would be invalided out and go home to his wife and kids instead of lying here like a chunk of rancid meat while we all gape at him hopelessly.'

'You can stow that kind of talk!' I growl harshly. 'You know as well as I do that the doctors gave him a clean bill of health. Martingale had to accept their word.'

We are stopped in the passage, talking in heavy whispers while the gurgling sound of Jennings's laboured breathing permeates the atmosphere.

'Naval quacks have malingering on the brain these days; especially when it comes to submariners,' snarls Tod. 'It is all too simple to diagnose a pain in the gut as the result of a man losing his nerve.'

As he starts to turn away I grab at his arm and hold him facing me. 'It's easy to talk after the event, Cooper. We sent him back to the doctor twice, and Falstaff even went to see the surgeon himself. They said that there was nothing wrong with him physically – what would you have done if you had been the skipper?'

He doesn't answer, and when I release his arm he goes off with his head down. I watch him go with a growing anger inside me. How bloody easy it is for him to criticise when he has not got responsibility for running the boat.

As the forenoon progresses Jennings obliges us all by slipping into unconsciousness. Anyone can see that he is dying, and the most we can do now is make sure that his air passage is kept open, clean him up from time to time, and hope that he doesn't wake up. By nightfall, when we go to diving stations for surfacing we are all wishing that he would get on with it, and not just lie there like an inert lump, taking up space and infecting everyone with his unsavoury presence.

He dies during the night without too much fuss or bother. We give him a final clean up, plug up the holes, and stow him aft amongst the steering and hydroplane gear with a blanket over his corpse. If we are lucky we shall get him back to Malta within fifty hours, and he will not make things too unpleasant before we arrive. If not, then Martingale is going to have to consider burying him at sea, for a submarine swimming through tepid seas is not the ideal mortuary.

*

Fifty hours is far too optimistic, for we find ourselves running into the Skerki Bank at nightfall on the third day, and because Martingale has no wish to negotiate the minefield on the surface we take time to charge our batteries fully before setting off for the shallows. We run along at about five knots with a running charge, moving in to hug the North African coast when we dive before dawn. The skipper intends to stay close to the shore until we are well past Cape Bon and to the south of Sousse. After that, if our luck holds good, we can surface for a while to top up the batteries in readiness for a run eastwards on our next leg. We must take our time now. If necessary spend the whole of the following day dived; running along on one motor at our slowest speed, until we can surface for the final sprint for home.

When Martingale calls me to the wardroom, it is to express his concern about the body in the humid atmosphere of the after-ends. It is quite obvious that this new plan will add another full day to our schedule, and the corpse is going to begin to decompose quite quickly. 'We cannot afford to wait too long, sir,' I explain. 'It looks as though we are going to spend most of our time dived, and I reckon that there is a sweet, sickly smell when I go through the after bulkhead. If we had an empty torpedo-tube we could stick him in that, and he would probably keep until we reach Malta. As it is, however, I think we should think about burial at sea.'

He has to agree, and with look-outs on full alert we shut down the diesels for a few minutes and heave to with the loom of the Tunisian coast just visible to the south. Martingale reads the service by the aid of a shaded torch while a token number of the lads muster on the casing to see Jennings off into the next world. Jumbo has made a neat job of sewing the body up in his hammock, and weighted it down with a 4-inch shell – compliments of the Navy. The corpse slides down over the ballast tank and enters the sea with hardly a splash, and we all turn inboard once more, trying not to show the relief we feel at having got rid of this encumbrance.

Before we reach the bridge a look-out reports in a hushed voice, 'I can hear something, sir!'

We tense and listen too. Above the soft slop of the bilges comes the unmistakable mumble of idling diesels puttering away somewhere between us and the coast. Martingale keeps his voice to a hoarse whisper as he orders us up over the top, and once all the spare bodies have gone below he calls down through the Asdic voice-pipe, asking for a search on the shore-side. When they do not reply he fumes at the helmsman, 'Tell the first lieutenant to get a man on the hydroplanes at once. It should have been done automatically the moment that we shut down the diesels.'

After a moment there is a squawk from the voice-pipe. 'Who's that?' he demands angrily.

'Trump, sir.'

'Well, Trump. Carry out an all-round sweep – report what you hear – and in future close up immediately the diesels shut down, without being told. Understand?'

'Aye aye, sir,' comes the subdued response. Then after a moment: 'HE on the starboard beam, sir. Green nine five. It sounds like diesel.'

'Could it be a submarine?'

'Yes, sir. There is no propeller noise. She could be charging batteries.'

'Or it could be an E–boat lying in wait for someone like us to happen along,' comments Martingale. 'Lurking in coves is one of their favourite pastimes.'

'Does a U–boat rate as a capital target, sir?' asks Subby in a whisper.

'In my book it does,' snaps Martingale with an edge to his voice. 'If we could hear more than one engine I would say there was a group of E–boats sitting there, lying doggo, but one engine chuckling away is another matter.' He taps indecisive fingers on the wooden capping, then brings his fist hard down with a bang that makes me start. 'Clear the bridge! We'll dive and creep in for a look-see.'

I raise my eyebrows to the heavens. Here we go again! Sod the orders! They state quite clearly that he must ignore all else in his effort to get the supplies to Malta, yet he uses precious time to investigate a noise that could recoil on us. We slide down without the klaxon this time, doing it all on slow time so that there is no tell-tale disturbance on the surface from the vents. Trump keeps his reports coming as we glide on down to thirty feet and point the bow towards the sound. Martingale sticks to the big, binocular periscope, risking its larger wake in order to get an early sight of whatever is making that sound.

'Five thousand yards – four thousand yards – three thousand yards.' Trump reels off the descending ranges with cool precision until it is down to a mile, and still that unassuming diesel putters away contentedly, oblivious to the rest of the war. There is a new note in the HSD's voice when he reports, 'Fifteen hundred yards, sir – and I am not so sure it is a submarine now.'

Martingale peers through the lenses, training the periscope either side of the bearing. 'Keep listening, we should pick her up soon.'

'One thousand yards – nine hundred yards.' It must be black up there, and the shore makes a dark backdrop. I feel the tension growing. The eye of the 'scope is just above the surface, hardly higher than the head of a swimmer. I can almost smell the tension now, and I force myself to concentrate on the depth-gauge.

Suddenly Trump's voice fills the control room. 'New HE, sir. One, two, three bearings. Fast diesel coming in fast!' There is no hiding the alarm in his tone.

Falstaff's breath hisses out through his teeth. 'Bastards!' he spits, echoing our thoughts as we realise how we have been coaxed into a neat little trap. That single boat with the puttering diesel was the decoy, and we have swallowed the bait hook line and sinker. Now her mates are coming alive in their hide-outs where they were lying with engines stopped, gloating as they listened to our screws driving us into the fold like a meek little lamb.

'Port thirty – hard dive – group up – full ahead together!' The orders come fast as we turn back towards the open sea. There is no subtle way of wriggling out of this one, just turn smartly and run like hell; and running like hell for a dived submarine adds up to ten knots, if we are lucky, and it will take several minutes to attain even that pedestrian pace. The hydroplanes are set to 'hard dive' and Falstaff is pushing all the spare blokes forward to weight down the bow in an effort to increase the diving angle. We are going down as fast as the screws and our willpower can drive her.

Pray that just this once they get it wrong. Hope that some incompetent bastard will fumble the settings on the depth-charges, or they will over-run us in their excitement. Anything that will grant us a few extra moments to think of something.

Now we can hear the propeller. No need for Trump to reel off ranges now, for the awful truth drums into our brains like a hammer. They have us dead to rights, and they know it. We can almost see their gloating eyes focused on the eggshell hull as they come in.

'One hundred and fifty feet!' Jumbo calls out the depth to remind Falstaff that we are heading towards the bottom fast. A twisting, diving turn towards the seabed as fifty-eight blokes hold their breath and pray.

When it comes it is beyond anything we can imagine. Trump snatches his headphones away with a yell as the charges thunder and crash about out ears. The boat rocks and shudders as though she is in agony. She is a live thing now. I have been through it before, but each time is the first time when it is as bad as this. Maybe it is the closeness of the land that exaggerates the noise. I can feel the slamming pressures on my skull as *Tarantula* gives a sickening lurch. She bucks and heaves, then slumps over to one side with a bow-down angle. The madness shuts in on us. It would be so easy to scream back at it, but I am the coxswain and I must sit with my hands gripped on the hard steel of the control, watching the needles swing relentlessly past one hundred and fifty feet.

'Take off the dive,' I tell myself. 'Pretend that you have some sort of control over this monster.' The bubble drifts aft on the clinometer. We are taking a nose-dive, and there is nothing any simple-minded man can do about it. Both 'planes come to 'full rise'. The needles swing past one ninety – two hundred – two hundred and ten, and all we can do is watch them as Trump reports in a dull, lifeless voice. 'New HE approaching – range decreasing – Depth charges!'

We hit the bottom like a sledgehammer. Everyone is sent

sprawling. She lifts, rolls, and crashes down with her tail sticking up for a moment before it settles with a gravelly crump as the next batch of depth charges detonate about us.

It makes no difference if anyone screams this time, for no one will hear it above the reverberations of this exploding hell, and there is no shame in screaming any more as the loose cork rains down and the lights flicker and die. There is water flooding in through the periscope flange, and Guns is holding his faithful old bucket beneath his voicepipe as it begins to leak profusely. From fore and aft reports are coming in; some good – some bad, and amazingly the hull remains intact as the nightmare goes on.

With all unnecessary machinery shut down we go into depth-charge routine. There is nothing more to do but sit tight and wait it out while they prowl about up top, although the hypocrites amongst us ask God to forgive the neglect of the past, and promise a renewed religious verve if he will just see us through this lot.

They have probably dropped a marker, but they are not absolutely certain of our exact position, for they make no full-patterned attacks. Instead, they drop the odd one just to let us know that they are still around, and to keep our nerves on edge. They know full-well that all they have to do is wait until our air gives out.

'What are you doing here, Perry?' The navigator's hoarse whisper makes everyone look in the direction of the forward bulkhead to see the scruffy torpedoman standing there with his thin body like an inverted plum-line as he balances against the lean of the boat. 'Oh no!' I think to myself. 'Not Clump!' He is the last person I would expect to crack.

Martingale intervenes. 'What is it, Perry?'

'Are we gonna stay dahn 'ere fer long, sir?'

'Several hours I should think. Why?'

Clump shuffles his big boots. 'Well, sir. On me last boat we used ter make a cup o' char when we was bein' depth-charged. I thought it might be a good idea.'

For a moment we all stare at the reprobate as he pleads with his captain. I could almost weep for the unpredictable young sod. Martingale grins. 'Why not? How do you intend doing it without making a noise?'

Clump shrugs his bony shoulders. 'Awe, me an' the chef'll manage, sir. The water is almost boilin', an' we can make up some fannies and pass 'em through the boat.'

'Go ahead then, but if you drop so much as a teaspoon I'll send you up to apologise to the Ities – understood?'

As Clump moves off another charge explodes near enough to rattle our teeth. 'All right, you bastards!' my mind tells them. 'Keep it up, but right now we are taking time off for tea.'

Seven

Clump, a couple of stokers and the cook perform miracles as they brew up enough tea for everybody and serve it out with a kind of silent ballet routine when they move from one compartment to the next. We watch their antics, enthralled at the way the big-footed torpedoman manipulates his heavy boots while balancing against the slope of the deck. We are by no means unique in serving tea during a depth-charge attack; some boats make a ritual out of it, and it brings a momentary period of light relief, even though we cringe at times when we remember how awkward Clump can be when he is not trying.

Now and then Trump makes a report to remind us of our tormentors prowling about up top, waiting to pounce the moment we betray ourselves. Maybe we should just stay where we are and allow our senses to become dulled through lack of oxygen, then we could drift off into the next world in a state of sublime euphoria. Another cup of tea, and seven hours later Martingale confirms my thoughts. 'They are waiting until daylight to make a concentrated attack,' he whispers. 'We are lying in less than two hundred feet of clear water, and anyone who has made a trip in one of those glass-bottomed sponge-fishing boats will know what that means. They will not require their hydrophones to pinpoint our position once the sun comes up. With the help of their chums in the Air Force they can pound us to scrap at their leisure.'

He pauses for a moment as he stares down at his watch. 'We cannot afford to just sit here and wait for their convenience. I intend to stick it out for one more hour in case some sort of miracle turns up; maybe the Seventh Cavalry will come charging over the hill.' He receives a muffled chuckle from those nearest to him for his weak attempt to lighten the atmosphere, but even if we were not restricted no one feels in a mood for laughing. In any case his words have to be relayed in hoarse whispers to each end of the boat, and the whole thing loses its point by the time it reaches the blokes crouched up in the forward or after ends.

'I am not going to mince words,' he goes on. 'We would not last five minutes if we tried to go up and fight it out on the surface, and we can do no more than ten miles at any speed with what we have left in our batteries. So, it is Hobson's choice, I'm afraid. One hour from now I will lift *Tarantula* off the bottom and sprint away for a few minutes, hoping to catch them off-guard. After that we'll go to "silent running" again, and try to find a patch of high density water to hide under.' He turns to Falstaff. 'These are the moments when I wish that we were supplied with the *Pillenwerfer* like our German colleagues.'

He leaves a silence in the boat that is almost tangible when he stops whispering. We know that it will take more than a canister of air-bubbles to get us out of this mess. Those blokes up top know where we are, and the moment they hear us bleeding air into the tanks they will be on us like a ton of bricks. A sprint to a submarine means a slow acceleration to something like nine or ten knots, and he is fooling no one. It is the classic nightmare situation for the likes of us: trapped close inshore, with nowhere to hide, while expert sub-killers prowl about upstairs. It registers in every face as we settle down to wait for the inevitable.

'Tis now the very witching time of night, when churchyards yawn and hell itself breathes out contagion,' quotes Falstaff again across my shoulder, and I wish him and his quotations to hell.

I no longer look at my watch. The minute hand is spinning out of control now; racing towards doom-time as though it has a death-wish. Instead, I turn my mind inwards to saner thoughts, but the more I try to concentrate on my home and family the more they paint pictures of Laura and the chintzy little café where we sat together on that autumn, Scottish day, with the dancing white-caps and the sad wind just outside the window. I wonder if Martingale spares a thought for her between trying to work out how to save his boat. The funny thing is that I have no twinges of jealousy when I pair them up.

It seems perfectly natural to put them together, and they have become like treasured possessions to me. I have become absorbed in their future as I would become absorbed in the main characters in a romantic novel, watching them overcome all their inhibitions and cock-ups to make a go of it in the end. Much as I like her style and looks I tell myself that it goes no deeper, and I have known from the start that she is not for me. Yet I feel intensely involved with them; almost as though I was fighting for my own future. Sometimes I think that the last person I will ever understand is myself.

A scurry of water skirls through the casing above my head. The dribble still runs down the long, honey-coloured shaft of the periscope into its well, but there is nothing more we can do about that for the moment; it will have to wait until we get to Malta – *if* we get to Malta. Most of the other leaks have been stopped, although the gun-layer still uses his bucket from time to time, with a wad of cotton-waste in the bottom to kill the sound when his mouthpiece spews half a pint of water every now and again. It is as if there is a small reservoir in the pipe that floods up until it spills over at regular intervals. There is a tangy, rust-flavoured smell in the boat as we try not to count the seconds that pass. I hoist my half-filled mug and find the tea cold. It has an oily scum on it, but my mouth is dry, and I swill some of it round and swallow.

Somewhere a man attempts to stifle a cough and succeeds only in producing an explosion of sound that draws a circle of condemning stares from his mates. I look down at my hands as they grip the steel rim of the hydroplane wheel. They are grimy and hard, like the metal; as though I am part of the beast that dominates our lives. I wonder if there is anyone thinking or caring about us as we sit here, deep down amongst the fishes, cut off from our own kind in this cigar-shaped bastard. Cut off from light and air in our own small capsule, steeped in our own stink while the claustrophobic tension builds.

'New HE – bearing red one seven five!' reports Trump to shake me out of my reverie.

'More E–boats?' queries Martingale glumly.

'No, sir. Heavier stuff this time. A mixture of reciprocating engines and turbines.'

If I move my head slightly I can see the skipper's face in the big dial of my depth-gauge. He is staring towards the Asdic cabinet as though he is forming a picture in his mind. 'A convoy?' he asks thickly.

Trump will not be rushed. He listens intently for a few seconds before he turns his head to peer out into the control room. 'Yes, sir. Almost certainly a convoy. About eight thousand yards and closing. I'm surprised I didn't hear it sooner.'

'I'm not,' declares the navigator from his chart-table. 'They have rounded the headland at Kelibia; hugging the coast just as we did. It is a favourite trick, and a well-trodden route for Mussolini's convoys. The shore must have cut off the sound.'

'The E-boats have started their engines!' reports Trump, gripping his earphones close to his skull.

'Not surprising,' says Martingale bluntly. He no longer needs to whisper, for he goes on to growl, 'They will come after us now. It is time we made a move. Blow ones, threes and fives – sixty feet – group up – full ahead together – port ten – steer two seven zero!'

Tarantula comes alive as high-pressure air roars into the tanks. She rocks, hesitates, then comes upright. 'Stop blowing!'

Martingale is gambling on the E-boats maintaining their deep settings on their charges as out depth-gauge needles sweep anti-clockwise.

'Fast HE approaching at attacking speed, sir!'

We swallow our bile and tense once more as we hear the mounting beat of the screws growing until it fills every corner of the boat. The skipper waits until the sound is right above our heads and every nerve stretched until it sings before he orders, 'Starboard thirty – flood ones, threes and fives!'

That holds her at sixty feet with neutral buoyancy while the next pattern roars and thunder beneath the keel. Everyone's breath hisses out when we realise that we have got away with it again as the enemy gets it wrong.

'Port ten!' snaps Martingale. 'We'll head straight for the convoy.'

Before we have time to recover from that piece of unwelcome news he confounds us all by adding bluntly, 'Stand by to surface – stand by numbers three, four, five and six tubes!' A dozen pairs of startled eyes goggle at him, wondering if he has finally cracked.

'Gun action, sir?' asks Falstaff in a tight voice.

'No, there will be no time for that. It's all or nothing now. Whatever we do they have us by the balls, so we will do what they least expect. I want full speed on the diesels the moment we open the hatch. We will run straight for the convoy – it is still dark and confusing up top, and the sea is building, so hopefully, there will be a period of uncertainty between the two forces when we broach. The E–boats will have us between them and the convoy while they recover their senses and decide whether to risk hitting one of their own ships when they open fire. We'll fire a spread of torpedoes at random to scatter the convoy, and dive underneath them while they are trying to sort themselves out.'

'Jesus!' exclaims a hidden voice.

'Yes, we will probably need him too,' comments Martingale drily.

'Fast HE closing on red four five, sir!' comes Trump's sobering voice.

'We'll have to put up with one more run,' declares Martingale coldly. 'I will wait until he is almost on us, then swing back to starboard and go for the convoy. 'Flood Q – one hundred and fifty feet!'

Down we go in a hurry, with Falstaff reeling off the increasing depth. 'One hundred – one hundred and ten – one hundred and twenty – '

The shock hits the soles of my feet, and the boat reels and bucks as tremendous forces lift her bodily to the ear-splitting detonations that numbs the mind. Dust and corking fill the control room as Falstaff falls across me and a roaring sound slogs my ears. I get the feeling my head is about to cave in with the sheer pressure of it. Someone makes a sound that is a cross between a scream and gurgle, but it is swallowed by two more monstrous bellowings from outside. *Tarantula* rolls her beam-ends over, and there is nothing to do but hold on while the lights flicker, die, then come alive again as the emergency ones cut in automatically. Thank God for a new, well-built boat! God bless the blokes at Vicker's for putting all their skill into her. The strong, acrid stench of the batteries mixes with the stagnant stink of stirred-up bilges and freshly exposed rust as we rock to the jangle of loose gear.

'How many charges do those bastards carry anyway?' pleads a plaintive voice from somewhere.

'Keep silence!' yells Martingale. 'Starboard twenty – hold those damage reports until we surface – steer zero five zero!' He turns to Falstaff. 'If you have ever wished confusion to your enemies, do so now.'

'This is a deed of dreadful note,' quotes the first lieutenant.

'Surface!'

Tarantula climbs as though she senses the madness of the occasion. Hoisting her long snout out of the ocean with white water spewing from her drain holes, she hangs for a moment before she crashes down to an even keel, heaving the rest of her black body awash as Martingale knocks off the second clip and thrusts the hatch back onto its latch. He is alone on the bridge, for Bunts is ordered to remain below at the foot of the ladder in case something happens to the skipper. If need be he will shut down and leave Martingale up top in order to save the boat.

Falstaff signals aft to tell the engine room to engage the clutches and feed compressed air through cam-operated distributors to the cylinders. They choke, stutter, then rumble into rhythm, gathering speed until they are thundering flat out to push us headlong into the heavy swell. The boat loses her wallowing motion and plunges into a body of water that sends a shudder through the hull.

Damage reports are coming in from all parts of the boat, telling of loose flanges, leaking pipes and seams, and a certain amount of battery damage, but nothing to put us out of action. Already the men are putting their sections in order with makeshift paddings and clamps. 'Fire three, four, five and six tubes!'

Subby clicks the knobs on his annunciator, and up forward Tod responds immediately.

I feel the speed building as the diesels get into full stride. They suck a gale of fresh air into the boat to chill the control room. I fancy that I hear the sound of gunfire, but it could just as easily be the crunch of heavy seas on the casing. She rears, holds, then plunges down into a trough. In the seven or eight hours we have been on the bottom the weather has deteriorated considerably, and there is a full gale blowing up top. It is a bonus for us, because it makes life harder for those gunners trying to balance on their jumping decks, and peering through their wet sights into a wind-lashed ocean. It may explain why they made such a hash of locating us the moment we moved, for the noise of the storm must confuse their hydrophones.

There are lucky and unlucky skippers, and Martingale seems to fall into the former category. Who else could whistle up a full gale to cloud the sky and hide our shape with white spume and spray just when we needed it? I have never blessed the weather with so much fervour as I do now. I can visualise *Tarantula*'s sleek shape half-hidden in a swelter of wild ocean as the enemy recovers from the shock of seeing us suddenly appear on the surface. The sky will split apart with the incandescent glare of starshell and rocket flares, but the E–boats will be bucketing madly in the blinding spray as their gunners try to hit our low profile. In the convoy there will be panic as someone spots the tracks of our torpedoes homing in, and merchantmen will take sudden avoiding action while their escorts charge about trying to run down the source of those tracks.

That is the picture we hope for. In reality the cold truth is that *Tarantula* has never been so naked and vulnerable. She is in the centre of an arena filled with vengeful antagonists vying with each other for the chance to blow her to bits. The strident scream of the klaxon saves me from more of these unsavoury contemplations. The diesels cut out and the ERA's fingers dart across his diving-panel. Martingale's feet clatter down the ladder, and we slide quickly down into a trough, roll to another heavy sea, then go down and down, even as the deep rumble of an explosion comes.

He must have cut it fine, for already we can hear the churning screws, and we brace ourselves for yet another pounding. 'One fifty feet!' orders Martingale before his shoes hit the deck. Those oncoming screws are beating with the slow, methodical pulse of a merchant ship as she crosses over us like a passing shadow.

'Group up – slow ahead port – silent running!' The noise dies. Once more we sneak along at snail's pace, with just enough steerage way to control the boat. The Italians have not got the sophisticated Asdic gear that we have. They must rely on their hydrophones, and at this moment half a dozen merchantmen are churning the water to drown out the small sound that we make. In fact, we are in no worse a position than a boat which has made a normal attack on a convoy. Dangerous, but not critical. Infinitely better off than we were a few moments ago. Just to add to the turmoil Trump reports breaking up noises.

We can scarcely accept our good fortune as Martingale orders a change of course that takes us out on a long leg towards the east. Trump reports diminishing disturbances astern, and we resist the temptation to soak up more energy by increasing speed. We have a boatful of air, and if we conserve battery power at two to three knots we can creep away quietly. It will take us ten hours to cover twenty miles, but who cares as long as they leave us in peace to lick our wounds? Every minute puts more distance between them and us, and that is all we care about.

As though to turn the screw a stealthy sound runs down the length of the hull, and a new, sickening feeling grips my insides. 'Take it easy,' warns Martingale quietly. 'It may not be what you think. In this area long strands of bladderwrack floats up to incredible length, and it could be that. Not mine moorings.'

We have to believe him. We desperately want to believe him. But we are only half convinced. Yet as the minutes tick by and the stealthy fingers continue to pass harmlessly down the sides we get to accept the serpentine, insiduous touch and become immune to it. There is an easing of tension, as though the depth-charges blasted away all imagination, so that we can blot out visions of mooring wires caught up in the hydroplane guards, dragging the small, black orbs down toward the thin hull, with their horns waiting to make contact.

Damage is slight. The periscope flange continues to weep, and the well is gradually filling, but that must wait until we get into harbour so that experts can have a look at it. Meanwhile our own skilled men are shutting valves or tightening nuts to isolate or stop leaks throughout the boat. We can see the sense of the bolted-down escape hatches now. Who needs them? Everyone knows that when the crunch comes it is highly unlikely that anyone will have time to make one of those controlled escapes so religiously taught in the practice tank at Gosport. Better to seal us down tight than to have a hatch that can jump out of its lugs when the depth-charges come. I ask permission to serve the rum. There is a quiet sort of elation that comes only when men have been reprieved from the death sentence.

By nightfall we are clear of the minefield and skirting another one that surrounds Malta as we round the southern tip; past Filfla, the rock blasted so often in peacetime by battlewagons as they exercise their massive guns, sometimes with a floating audience of expensive tourists ensconced on the upper-deck of an ocean liner.

Past Marsaxlokk Bay, and northward toward the swept channel that takes us in through the gap between Fort St Elmo and Dragot Point into Marsamxett Harbour, to find our berth alongside the submarine base at Manoel Island. *Tarantula* rolls like a bucket when we surface astern of the escort that leads us through the minefield, but no one cares. There is a fresh, clean feel to the draught that comes down the conning-tower as we follow her through. Each night the enemy comes to seal up this channel, and the navy is hard put to keeping it clear of magnetic and floating mines. They have had to introduce new, drastic methods to keep it open; even resorting to blasting the way clear with depth-charges. Yet, still the little corvette finds a couple to blow up as she sweeps ahead of us. We are all much relieved when we finally sidle snugly alongside the floating pontoons in Lazzaretto Creek.

Once we are secured from harbour stations and Martingale rings off the motors I glance ashore where I see a group of senior officers standing on the smooth-stoned jetty, waiting to greet the skipper as he bounces across the gang-plank with his documents clasped in one hand. Prominent amongst them is the portly shape of none other than our prime persecutor, Captain Boxwell, wearing a scowl on his chubby red face. He should have been a thousand miles away in Alex according to what we were told at Gibraltar, and somehow I sense that his presence here bodes ill for our future. As I stare down at him he raises his eyes and we meet eyeball to eyeball for a few unguarded seconds before he turns hastily away. I know in that instant that he can hardly wait to get his claws into the skipper for deviating from his orders. The lads in the boat may have forgiven Martingale for taking them into the lion's den, but he is going to face the music when that fat bastard gets him on his own.

The moment we are tied up things begin to happen. We have two injured men who have to be taken to hospital at Mtarfa, for Bhigi is almost out of commission because of the bombing. The specialists who come on board tell us that the Germans and Italians are stepping up their raids, and as *Tarantula* presents such an inviting target for them she will have to lie submerged for long periods during daylight hours. Therefore Falstaff and I arrange for half the crew to go ashore into the barracks, while the remainder have the unenviable duty of manning the boat while she sits in the pellucid water when the enemy blasts hell out of the island. One glance at the gaping holes in the buildings, and the rubble that strews across the streets is enough to put us in the picture. There is an average of two to three raids a day now, and three at night. Hitler and Il Duce have decided to pummel the natives into submission, and they are putting all their effort into it.

The mind refuses to hold on to bad memories. People who have been in horrifying car crashes will recall nothing afterwards, although in the ensuing years some vague recollection may filter through. So it is with us. Our senses are already dulled to the terror we lived through as we lay on the sea-bed, weighed down by the crushing pressures of the ocean while the thunder of depth-charges roared in our ears. Those visions are already relegated to deep recesses in the backs of our minds, where they will do least damage, and Malta allows small respite to dwell on such contemplation anyway.

The island has a besieged air about it. The soft yellow stone that can almost be sliced with a butter-knife soaks up punishment like blotting-paper, and people learn to live their lives from boltholes. They have set up small communities, self-contained, with their own little store, a couple of pubs, a priest, and a shrine.

The winter of 1941/42 is a dank and dismal one. It saps the spirit and the strength of the people as the simmering cauldron engulfs us all. Packs of abandoned dogs search about for scraps left over by the hungry Maltese and find little to fill their grumbling bellies. Known as the 'Black Winter', the first real meaning of siege is beginning to seep into the minds of everyone as they try to sustain some kind of normal existence under the continuous bombardment. New diets are concocted, like the *Soppa ta L'armla* (widow's soup). Made with anything you can find growing in a back yard, with one egg dropped in at the last moment to add strength just before it is consumed. Add a pinch or two of ricotta cheese for flavour, if you are lucky, and it makes a meal of sorts. They call it 'widow's soup', because even the poorest housewife can afford some version of it.

What goes on behind those dark, leathery faces? The 'Joes', or the 'Malts' as our lot call them, in their loose dockyard-matey overalls and tatty caps. The lightermen with their cloth headbands, humping sacks of spuds across open hatches on springy planks. The olive-skinned doe-eyed mothers with babies in their arms who will not fill out to become blousy as quickly as they normally do out here. Standing or squatting outside doorless entrances to shelters, staring out at passers-by with resigned faces. Their enemy is the Italians, more than the Germans, for they feel betrayed by their close neighbour, and in any case, they have always been resolute in their independence from the overbearing authorities from the north.

Most have been evacuated into country villages where they must learn to live like peasants again, for there is a marked difference in Malta between the town dweller and the villager who still retains an ageless independence. They speak a language of their own, more Arabic than anything else, although the wealthy folk who inhabit the opulent parts of Sliema and other residential areas consider it beneath them to use it, preferring to speak English or Italian. The time is coming when the enemy will pay more attention to these selected places, however, and war can be a great class leveller.

Those who choose to brave the ceaseless clamour, dirt, and rubble in the quaking streets, dodging falling debris and bearing the cacophony of the 'box barrage' set up to defend the ships in the harbour, live out their days like rodents. They emerge from their holes only to forage for food, kerosene, scraps of timber from bombed houses, and most precious of all to some – soap. Dockyard workers learn to drop tools at a second's notice several times a day to scamper for cover, although some toil right through everything in underground workshops carved out of the soft rock.

No wonder few matelots bother to cross the causeway from Manoel Island for a run ashore. Apart from a fair chance of having your head blown off, the whole atmosphere is one of abject depression that no amount of local hooch can dispel. We work hard and long to make the boat ready for sea, for by mutual agreement we have decided that Malta is a good place from which to escape. So when Martingale stumps across the plank with a determined look on his face our hopes rise, and we gather round in anticipation, waiting for him to tell us that we are about to shove off again.

He soon puts paid to those aspirations as he explains that it will take at least four days to repair the periscope flange, for both top and bottom castings have to be taken apart, and this can only be done on the surface. 'It means,' he adds, as though he enjoys taking the wind out of our sails, 'that we can no longer enjoy the luxury of diving all day, and I have arranged for the people on shore to provide a smoke-screen.'

'Oh, goody goody!' mutters someone almost out of earshot. 'If Jerry don't get us with 'is bombs we'll choke to fuckin' death!'

If Martingale hears he makes no comment, but goes on steadily: 'I shall call a meeting of heads of departments tomorrow morning for a situation report, so have all your facts ready. I want detailed damage reports, and list of all the stores and supplies we require. Whether we'll get them is another matter.'

He begins to turn away, then hesitates as though he has decided to let us in on something. 'By the way, you may pass this message to everyone. The explosion we heard just before we dived under the convoy was an ammunition ship going up. They say you could see the glare forty miles away. That, and some very useful information recovered from the schooner, is more than enough to compensate for the trauma we suffered at the hands of those E–boats. Congratulations, everyone. I'll see you in the morning.'

He scrambles up the hatch, leaving behind a thoughtful

silence until Falstaff comments, 'Well, what are we all standing about doing nothing for? There is a hell of lot to do, and we'd better get on with it.'

The small group breaks up as we slope off to break the news to our different departments. A few youngsters show delight at the news of the sinking, but mostly there is a subdued reaction from those who remember how close we came to bloody disaster, especially when most of us know that the skipper broke every rule in the book to get us into that situation. Not many are taken in by Martingale's outwardly cheerful disposition. I am sure he has been well and truly verbally chastised for his actions. However, like most of the senior hands I also know that if it was not for law-breakers like him we would have fewer successes in our efforts to stop Rommel's supplies getting through. There are many like him who would never have got a command in peacetime, because they are mavericks, with minds of their own, and a bloody-minded attitude towards needless bullshit. To be a good skipper these days you need brains and imagination, and that doesn't come anywhere near to blind obedience. Nor can they be recognised by their flamboyant mannerisms or aggressive attitude, for they are often quiet, unassuming men with a job to do. It requires more than panache to win a war. It is results that count, not the art of catching an admiral's eye at Divisions.

Tonight the sky is alive with stars when I come up top for a breather. The sandstone buildings are etched out in mellow indigo under a bright moon that hangs like a medallion in the velvet firmament above the black ramparts of the town. It is an open invitation to the Luftwaffe and Regia Aeronautica, and it is not long before they accept. As I go through the small archway that leads into the fort, the first wail of the siren howls its mournful message into the night, and its baleful moan is taken up by its colleagues until a full chorus fills the creeks and harbours. A Maltese steward comes wandering by, showing no sign of being in a rush to take cover. 'Where's the nearest shelter?' I ask him.

He grins white teeth at me and shrugs. 'No panic, chief! This is what you call a nuisance raid, just to make sure that we stay awake at night. They hit nothing but dirt, and stay high in the sky.' He prods a finger towards the north, where already the long, probing searchings are criss-crossing the night sky. 'It will be the Italians,' he explains as though that is reason enough to carry on as normal and ignore them. There is a contemptuous edge in his voice.

'You don't like the Italians?'

He spits into the gutter. 'I am Maltese. For many years the Italians have tried to make us part of them.' He spits again. 'Stupid! Only a few people speak the language, and since 1934 Maltese is our official written word. We do not have to lick the arse of Il Duce.'

The drone of bombers is almost overhead now, and the guns are banging away. He might be right about the bombs, but there is more danger of being hit by a piece of our own shrapnel. I can distinguish the pulsating rhythm of the Bofors amongst the heavier thump of the big guns. I decide to take shelter under the thick walls of the ancient fort.

Eight

There is a small office built into the outside wall of the fort next to the bos'n's store where we meet in the half-light like a lot of medieval conspirators, with our ringleader listening to our reports and divulging his schemes. It is almost as though our plans must be kept secret even from those we call our friends. He doesn't mention his interview with Boxwell, but it is clear to me that we are on some sort of probation, and the reputation we gained in Scotland has followed us out here.

'I want the boat ready in all respects to sail by Monday morning,' he tells us bluntly. 'You will inspect and service the four replacement torpedoes thoroughly, Cooper, and any that you have the slightest doubt about, let me know, and I'll see that we get them changed. There is a lot of old junk here, some of it dating back to the First World War. Guns! You will be happy to learn that I have cadged two extra Lewis guns. Their mountings are being welded into place tomorrow.'

He stares into our faces one at a time. 'We are going to work around the clock to make her ready on time: I'll tell you why the moment we get to sea. In the meantime, I want to know immediately if there are any snags that could cause delay. I shall be available day and night, and heaven help the man who decides that I should not be disturbed if he has something to report.' He takes a long, deep breath. 'Now is the time to voice any gripes you might have as a group. I'll be coming to talk to each of you individually as time goes by, but once this meeting breaks up there will be no more get-togethers.'

We give him our reports in turn, along with one or two requests. He makes notes, but promises nothing, for there are few spares in the island at the moment. It is a case of make do and mend until we get to Alex.

The replacement PO Tel has more reason to hate the Germans than most of us, for he comes from the Channel Islands, and his two schoolage lads were taken up to their local school in the dead of night, bussed down to a cattle-boat in the harbour with labels round their necks and a change of underwear, to be evacuated to England while their mother was having complications producing his third child. Up to now he doesn't know whether he is a new father or a widower.

His name is Mauger, and because some of us have a hard time pronouncing it, we all call him 'Froggy'. He doesn't seem to mind, in fact it pleases him, for as he says. 'I'm descended from Normans. One of my ancestors was the nephew of William the Bastard before he changed his handle to William the Conqueror when we overran you lot.'

He should be twice as despondent as Jennings was, but he isn't. He is just a very angry man. 'When I think of those grey-suited bastards strolling about my bloody island I'd like to hear the sods screaming when we plant a fish right where it hurts the most.' Whereas Jennings was an introverted bloke, ignored by most of us as he sat with his nose buried in a book, this bloke has no intention of being ignored. As Martingale introduces him we all have the same, uncharitable thought, that he has to be an improvement on the miserable sod we buried at sea.

It goes a long way toward dispelling any remaining niggles we might have about the way the PO's illness was not taken seriously. That kind of thing happens in the service. It is the responsibility of the quacks to decide if a man is spoofing or not, and if they get it wrong now and then, hard luck; it's just part of the game. Submarines are inhabited by young, healthy males with an underlying aversion to illness or shortcomings. We are a bit like wild animals and birds who will ignore, or even get rid of one of their own kind who falls below par and becomes an encumbrance to the remainder of the group.

When the meeting breaks up Martingale takes me to one side. 'The first lieutenant tells me that everyone is in good fettle, Grant. You are closer to them than we are; is that your opinion too? Don't pull any punches either. I have given them plenty to gripe about.'

He knows he can trust me to give him the truth with no frills.

'They are glad to be alive, sir. You got us into a jam, but you got us out of it; that's good enough for them. There is only one skipper in the boat, and if we cannot trust him the whole thing falls apart.'

'No gripes at all?'

'Only the usual drips. All officers are bastards to some blokes, and it is generally accepted that any decision taken by some bloke in an armchair back at base has to be a bloody shambles. Speaking for myself, I think you made a cock-up taking us in after that engine noise, but that's easy to say in hindsight. There are plenty of the other kind of skipper who never breaks the rules, but few blokes want to serve with them. I reckon submariners are a bunch of bloody pirates at heart, and they need a bit of a blackbeard in command.'

He grins widely. 'You don't mince words, do you?'

'I don't think you'd want me to do that, sir.'

He relaxes, and we walk together along the flagstoned jetty. 'I'd like you to do something for me.' He digs a hand into his pocket and pulls out a small parcel. 'It is personal. I want you to deliver this to a party we both know. She is in the Naval Operations Room at Lascaris, and you will require your paybook to get past the entrance. I have made arrangements, so you should have no difficulty.' He stops when he sees the look on my face. 'Don't be concerned. You are not playing Cupid. It is just a small token that I picked up to show my appreciation. I cannot possibly get away from the fort or I would give it to her myself.'

'Appreciation for what, sir?' I know that I am verging on insubordination, but this is personal, and I have to know if he is trying to use her again.

He looks away. 'I kept that diary back, and submitted only the documents we found to Captain Boxwell, because I knew he would try to block my report. There was a party, and Laura promised to get the diary to a person I know at headquarters. She will have a package for you when you see her.'

'She is sticking her neck out, isn't she, sir? I assume that Boxwell is still her boss?'

It is as though he hasn't heard, or doesn't wish to hear the implication behind my words. 'She is a brick, Grant. You know, I might even propose to the girl when we get to Alex.'

'Congratulations,' I say sarcastically. For all that I like this bloke, his sheer bloody arrogance where Laura is concerned riles me. I decide to change the subject. 'I thought the op's room was in St Angelo, sir?'

'Not any more. They have moved to underground chambers beneath the Lascaris Bastion. I will arrange a boat to take you around to Grand Harbour. If you go ashore at Customs House Steps it is only a few steps along the water-front to the entrance. The dungeons under Fort St Angelo are being used for another, more sinister purpose. No one knows what goes on down there, but there are a lot of strange, secretive bods moving about like moles, up to all sorts of skulduggery. Even if you can't get to see Laura in person, make certain that you deliver the package; it's all-important.'

'Aye aye, sir.' There seems nothing else to say. He makes it all sound so matter-of-fact; as though Laura is bound to react the way he wants, without question. Somehow I think it is going to take a lot more than this small offering to placate her.

It is Sunday before I get the opportunity to go to Grand Harbour, and we are no sooner through the pier-heads when the bombers arrive. The red flag goes up on the ramparts of Ricasoli while we are still making our way towards the landing, closely followed by a chorus of sirens. Our Maltese coxswain sets his swarthy face hard and holds on to his course, heading straight for the steps at Customs House, right opposite the imposing Fort St Angelo. We must have covered a third of the distance before the first undulating throb of engines drones in across Valletta. Every London schoolboy knows that sound, and can recognise it as distinct from the steady roar of our own aircraft. The mutter of guns grows with it; increasing in volume until the air vibrates with the sound. It reverberates from the cliffs and walls, to fill the harbour and kill the wind with its concussion. The surface is splattered with falling shrapnel, and at the moment we have more fear from that than enemy bombs. The stoker nudges his throttle in a vain attempt to coax another half a knot out of the engine.

The first planes come in shallow dives from the north, closely followed by another wave from the open sea. They are trying to split the barrage, but the shore-guns are set to provide a solid criss-cross pattern of fire, so that they weave an intricate lacework of lethal ironmongery, through which any low-flying hero of the Third Reich must penetrate to hit his target. Just before we thump alongside the steps a yellow-nosed, leopard-spotted Me109 skids across the harbour below the height of the battlements with guns spitting and engine screaming into a howling crescendo as the pilot hauls it up into a climbing turn through the man-made curtain of fire.

By now I am too busy scurrying across the stonework for cover to see the Junker 88s deliver their loads, and when I am snuggled hard into the small grotto with a few fellow survivors the whole scene is full of dust and smoke as the first phase of the raid comes to an end and the Stukas arrive to pick up the theme. The sour howl of their diving sirens joins the unholy racket as they tumble out of the sky like black hawks, with their noses aimed at the ships standing stark and naked at their moorings.

No one has told the Germans that the Junkers 87 dive bomber is outmoded and unsuitable to modern warfare. They are extremely vulnerable when they pull out of their dives and struggle to regain altitude. Slow and cumbersome, they rely on the skill of their pilots for success, and many of the crack ones of earlier days turned it into a terrifying weapon. However, the death toll was high, and now, in the hands of less experienced men it becomes less awesome, and our gunners and fighter-pilots have the upper hand. No longer do the defenders cringe at the sound of the diving sirens, and although the book says that their well-aimed bombs should find a target more often than their high-flying comrades, it takes nerves of steel to hold onto a dive when a hail of shrapnel is exploding in front of your eyes. They pull out early, release their bombs too soon or too late, and veer away from their targets when their nerves crack. Even when they do carry out their attacks well there is always that posse of fighters waiting on the sidelines to jump them as they emerge from the box-barrage to make for home.

To someone like me who has no experience of the nightmare it is beyond belief. It seems impossible that anyone can survive and get used to the insane bedlam, or the stink and the dust. Yet when I look at the faces of those who are sheltering with me I see no panic or real fear, and a couple of ten-year-old kids have to be told off for sticking their heads out to watch the show. These people have had their fear and panic pounded out of them. Their senses are numbed by incessant noise and outrage, and they are much more concerned about where the next meal is coming from. Compared to the raids on Britain the death-toll amongst the civilians is small, because the sandstone soaks up punishment like a sponge. When the Luftwaffe tried to have a go at Luqa airfield recently some of their pilots took the easy way out and unloaded their cargoes onto the nearby village. More than seventy houses were wrecked beyond repair, and many other severely damaged, yet, out of the mess, only one villager was killed, for they were hidden in shelters carved out of the rock by local stone-masons.

We emerge dusting ourselves down as the last aircraft drones away and the steady note of the all-clear wails across the walls. A pall of dust hangs on the static air, and seabirds take time to recover their voices, while human beings come out into the sunlight. Somewhere up French Creek flames are reaching up into a rising column of smoke, and there are people digging amongst the rubble of a ruin nearby, but there is a dogged acceptance as we each brush ourselves down and go our own way.

The Marine sentry takes a long time to study the picture in my paybook and compare it with the real thing before he consults a list of authorised visitors and allows me through. The moment I enter the inner door I come up against a barrier in the form of a high counter that barricades the inner caverns of this dank place. Everyone is as busy as hell pounding typewriters and shuffling papers, and I am totally ignored as I stand like a lost soul with my cap in hand, until eventually someone notices me.

As far as I'm concerned the whole scene changes when they carry my message through and Laura comes out looking fresh and smart in her crisp white blouse and dark skirt. 'Hello, Ben!' she greets in a voice that turns many heads. It is generally accepted that Wrens do not consort with anything with less than one gold ring on its sleeve. It is a sad fact that erstwhile shopgirls, bottle-washers and milkmaids take on airs and graces the moment they have passed their apprenticeship, and are usually accepted by matelots as officers' groundsheets. That probably maligns a large proportion of them, but once you have suffered at the hands of a jumped-up stores assistant, or a flouncy clerk in the paymaster's office, who seem to delight in keeping men standing about while they touch-up their nail-varnish or discuss last night's party, it is difficult not to tar them all with the same brush. Especially when the victim is a survivor from a sunken ship, having lost his kit, his mates, and his nerve, yearning only to get 'up the line' to his loved ones and never go to sea again. I know there are many of the other kind, and that they probably outnumber the rest, but most blokes only remember the haughty looks and turned-up noses.

'I have something for you,' I stammer like a sprog, and push the package across the counter, conscious of the eyes staring up surreptitiously from behind typewriters and telephones.

'Not here,' she smiles. 'Give me a few minutes, and I shall be off-duty. You will find a small tavern just along the road; about a hundred yards past the jetty. The proprietor is an ex-marine who manages to keep open right through the raids. We call him Uncle Jim. He will look after you while you wait for me.'

'I am supposed to collect a package from you.'

She grins. 'That is just his excuse for getting you to come. The package could easily have been sent by messenger.' There is only half a smile on her face now, and I can detect an underlying resentment in her voice. I slide out past the sentry to find that the dust has settled, and a blustery wind is bringing a fresh tang from the sea. All that remains of the flame and smoke in French Creek is a wisp of grey drifting across Corradino Heights. Several dghaisas beetle about as their owners lean into their oars and ply for trade. They look like ornate, miniature gondolas amongst the greys and yellows of their surroundings.

Uncle Jim has tattooed arms and a bunch of shrubbery growing out of his chest like barbed-wire. When he sets a glass down in front of me his huge frame cuts off the light from the wide entrance. 'Sods broke half me fuckin' crockery,' he grumbles deep down in his throat. 'You orf one of those submarines?'

I glance at the motif behind his head that warns of careless talk. 'That's right,' I answer weakly.

'Thought so. You blokes always 'ave a pong about yer, no matter 'ow much yer tries ter scrub it orf.'

'What's in this?' I ask, jabbing my thumb at the glass.

'What d'yer care. Maiden's water – witches' piss; it'll take away the stink and the noise. It deadens the mind and softens the soul.'

'Oh!'

'Change yer sex life that will. Especially good fer young sprogs: Those who are used ter three jerks and a spit. It turns 'em inter real performers.'

'I'm told you are called Uncle Jim,' I say doubtfully.

His grin widens. 'Yer bin talkin' ter that mob from the caves. I change my style fer them. They come in 'ere lookin' fer a father-figure and a bit of a giggle.' His face gets sober. 'God, yer ought to see the state of 'em sometimes. Eyes like piss'oles in the snow. 'Ands shakin' and lookin' like ghosts. Christ knows what they do to earn their bread, but it takes it out of 'em, and they come in 'ere ter laugh it orf.'

'You don't feed them this muck?'

His face gets defensive. 'Don't get too lippy about me stock. There is a bloody war on!'

I pull out a small medicine bottle and watch his eyes gloat as I twist off the top. 'That's bubbly!' he breathes in hushed reverence.

'Neaters!' I proclaim, enjoying the incredulous light in his eyes. 'I always take a bottle on shore in places like this. I don't want your rot-gut, and you look as though you could do with a nip.'

He reaches out a long arm and slaps another glass onto the table. 'I take back orl I ever said about fuckin' dabtoes,' he says with his lips slavering.

We go silent as I pour the dark-brown liquid with precision. It is not the moment for talk, and we both lift our glasses in mutual appreciation, savouring the fiery flavour as it burns its way down our gullets. That done, I top up with the remains of the bottle, and now we can relish it and talk.

'What are you doing here?' I ask after another sip. 'Don't the raids get you down?'

'Naw. This place is tucked well in under the cliff. They would 'ave ter blast their way through a hundred feet of rock ter get at me, and these days people look fer a bit of somethin' strong ter keep their nerves goin'.' He twiddles a chair and sits on it back to front with his huge arms resting on the back. 'Those bloody Stukas though. They used ter scare the shit aht of me, but now I can see 'em fer what they are – all wind and piss. Typical Teutonic they are. If they could the jerries would 'ave twenty stone Wagnerian opera singers straddled across the engine cowlin's with fire spurtin' from their tits, and singin' *Die Walküre!*' He changes tone. 'What am I doin' 'ere? I came 'ere donkey's years ago on the 'ood – the 'Mighty '*ood*', as they called 'er in those days. All ponced-up with gloss-paint and brasswork, lookin' like a Piccadilly tart. What a ship she was! Gin flowin' like water from 'er bilges. Orficers' cabins like rooms in a bag-shanty. We shagged our way round the world on that cruise, and when we got 'er back 'er innards were in such a state of bad repair she 'ad ter 'ave a refit.'

His eyes take on a nostalgic look. 'What a life! I came out shortly after that and found every bastard skint and out of work. So I up-sticks and comes aht 'ere, and I bin 'ere ever since. If I'm gonna starve, I thought I might as well do it in the sunshine. I found me a woman and got spliced. She was a little raver. Stank like a camel's crutch, but shagged like a rattlesnake. Between us we could turn the bedroom inter a disaster area in 'arf an hour. What's more she was a widow, and came complete with a sixteen-year-old daughter. What more could a man arsk for?'

I drain my glass and cock an eyebrow. 'Nothing, I suppose.'

He stares down at my empty glass as though making up his mind about something important, then makes a momentous decision. ''Ang on!' He goes over to the counter and delves beneath it, making sure his movements are well hidden from prying eyes. ''Ere!' he offers, setting a couple of bottles of blue label beer in front of me.

'Thanks,' I say with profound gratitude. The insipid liquid would make a Geordie cringe, but I know that I am privileged.

'You must have made an impression!' We swing to stare at her as she stands framed in the entrance. Immediately Uncle Jim's attitude undergoes a complete change. ''Ello, me dear,' he drools with a benign smile that would have met with Fagin's approval. 'Come an' sit dahn.. Yer lookin' tired.' He pulls his chair round the right way and flicks the seat with a towel. 'I'll make yer somethin' special.' He shambles off like an ageing bullock.

She giggles secretly. 'He thinks he has us all fooled, the old reprobate, but he is too old to be a menace any more, and we play back to him for fun.' She stops talking as he comes back with two tall glasses and an assortment of bottles. There are reds, yellows, blues and greens, plus a milky concoction that must provide the fire. He pours steadily while we watch fascinated as each layer remains in sequence without mixing at all – it is his speciality act.

'Try it,' she urges.

I'm a bit dubious, but when I sip it tentatively it tastes harmless enough; too syrupy for me, but I can see its merit. In any case they are not exactly spoiled for choice out here. I nod appreciation and he grins back proudly before sliding off to leave us on our own.

'Here!' I say, setting the small package in front of her.

She takes it delicately and plays with it a moment, as if she is reluctant to open it. After a moment she sighs and begins to strip away the wrapping. Inside is a small jeweller's case. 'Should I open it now?' she asks, looking at me.

'Why not?' 'The sod!' I'm thinking. 'He's made me play cupid after all!'

She hesitates as though she is half-inclined to leave it, then shrugs and opens the lid. We both gasp at what's inside. It is a silver brooch; and what a brooch! It is one of the most delicate pieces of fine-workmanship that I have ever seen. About an inch and a half long, it is an exact replica of an Admiralty-pattern anchor, with a dolphin twisted round the shank. He must have gone to great trouble to have it made especially for her, and at great expense. We both stare down at the intricate detail, and when I lift my eyes I can see she is moved. I get a sudden twinge. 'It's a masterpiece!' I choke.

She nods, and I swear that there is a tear swimming in her eye. Carefully she shuts the lid and replaces the case onto the table. The silences stretches for a bit, as though she can find no words to say what she is feeling. She snaps her head up smartly. 'The beast!' she exclaims, taking me aback. 'Don't you see what he is doing, Ben? He is playing with us. Asking you of all people to deliver his little bribe. Who does he think he is?' She is beside herself now, and she looks into my face. 'Who do you think you are? You have both made up your minds about me, haven't you? You are quite willing to play postman. I know he is your captain, Ben, but he doesn't own you.'

'It's not like that at all,' I protest. 'He has got all kinds of problems on his hands, or he would have come himself, believe me!'

'Don't kid yourself!' she bites back. 'There is no excuse for him to think that everyone will dance to his tune. He takes advantage, Ben – of everyone.'

'He is a good skipper.'

'That is not what they are saying in my office.'

'Boxwell's office, you mean. What the hell do they know? They've forgotten what it is like under pressure at sea.'

She relents a little, and leans closer. 'I shouldn't tell you this, Ben. As far as your captain is concerned he is on probation, and only the sinking of that ammunition ship, along with the recovery of the documents from the schooner, stopped them throwing the book at him. If Boxwell has his way he will lose his command and never get so much as a trawler again.' She leans back. 'I have probably said too much already, but you should know what you are letting yourself in for. Your captain has to prove himself, whatever the cost.'

I haven't the heart to argue anymore. How can she know what goes on in a boat? How can anyone know who hasn't experienced it? Martingale makes snap decisions all the time that affect the lives of fifty-odd other blokes. If we knew half the time what he is taking us into there would be a riot. That's why he is a skipper, and not a dozen others who all think they can do better. He takes the full weight of the boat twenty-four hours a day. It crowds in on his personal life and leaves no room for the niceties of convention. She should take him for what he is – blunt, totally committed to *Tarantula* and her crew.

Uncle Jim comes bustling in through the entrance. 'The flags are goin' up agin. If yer 'as somewhere ter go, yer better get movin' before it starts ter rain bombs agin.'

I look at her, and she nods her head. 'You'd better come with me,' she says urgently. 'I have no intention of being cooped up in those dungeons for a moment longer than I have to be, and there will be no boat for you until the raid is over. I have a small place and a ration of tea. Enough kerosene to boil up a kettle of water and some goat's milk. The sooner the Maltese invent cows, the better!'

I follow her out as the sirens tune up, and she leads me along the waterfront to where the road bends back on itself to zig-zag up the cliff. There is a row of thick-walled houses nestling into the rockface, and it would take a clever bomb to locate them. She ushers me through a tight little alleyway and the door to one of the houses opens for us. A small, dark-skinned girl peers out with worried eyes.

'You had better get along quickly, Mila,' urges Laura. 'Take care of your mother, and don't leave her until you are sure she is all right.'

The girl scuttles away, wrapping a scarf about her head as she goes. Everywhere you look the streets are emptying fast, in readiness for their next ordeal. Laura slams the door shut behind us. It is a neat, feminine place with small alcoves etched into the walls. I stare at a crucifix and she catches my eye. 'I rent it from the girl's family. Most of them have gone into the country, but mother stays put because she is crippled and cannot bear to leave her things behind. She lives with a relative close by, but if it was not for Mila she would go mad.'

She is busy with her utensils, and soon the old-fashioned smell of kerosene fills the room. We can ignore the growing tide of sound coming from outside, and the small cataracts of sand spilling from the nooks and crevices. The whole cliff seems to quake at times to the pulsating volume of noise, but we are determined that it will not intrude.

'This is nice,' I comment lamely, nodding at the walls.

'And illegal,' she grins. 'I have official quarters near Msida, but I have to have a place where I can be alone sometimes. You are most privileged, I'll have you know. Very few people know this place exists. Anyway,' she says, a little sadly, 'it is not for long. We are moving on to Alex shortly.'

She sets her cup down as a thunderous explosion shakes the house. A picture falls from the wall, and I swoop down to pick it up as the sour scream of a Stuka turns into a full-throttled roar as its big Juno tries to pull it out of its dive. For a moment the barrage increases to an incredible volume, making it impossible to talk. The noise slams into the building and destroys every other sensation as we stand together, trying to remain sane. We hear the engine sound stutter, choke, then turn into a scream of agony until it ends with a shattering explosion. The bedlam eases, and we look at each other. 'Good!' she says with a harsh glint in her eyes.

I nod slowly. 'That's one that won't come back.'

She shudders as though she feels a chill. 'God, I hate this bloody war!' It is a simple statement, full of petulence. All that is needed to turn it into a schoolgirl tantrum is for her to stamp her foot, and she knows it, for she looks at me and giggles.

Reaction sets in and in a moment we are laughing. The noise has died completely, and the steady wail of the All-clear sounds. Without thinking I lift my cup and take a sip, then spit it back. 'Strewth, it's full of dust!' and that brings another burst of silly laughter as the tension dies away.

'I'll make some more,' she offers in a moment of sanity.

'No,' I say soberly. I have lost my excuse for staying any longer now that the raid is over. 'I must go and catch my boat or they will have a patrol out looking for me.' But I make no move to go, and she comes round the table. 'Your uniform is very rough,' she says quietly.

'It's my number threes,' I explain with a lump in my throat. 'All my spare kit is on its way to Alex.'

Her fingers clutch at my sleeve and her face turns up towards mine. 'I've a good mind to make you take that damned brooch back to where it came from.'

'That wouldn't be right. I wouldn't know what to say.' I can hold back no longer. I bend to kiss her. God, it is so peaceful here, and she feels so good in my arms!

A while later she walks with me down to the jetty, where the steam pinnace lies alongside with its Maltese crew waiting to get away. The air is clean and bright, with a crisp breeze stealing in from the harbour-gate to ruffle the surface. I am feeling good, with no sense of time nor guilt. We hardly say a word as I wait my turn to board. We hardly notice a strange new atmosphere growing about us, until the crew of the pinnace suddenly stop their efforts to hurry us aboard and look towards the breakwater. People are moving away from the edge, and all eyes are focused in one direction. There is an air of expectation, like an audience waiting for the curtain to rise.

We move with them, shading our eyes to see what they can

see. There is a milky haze beyond the harbour, where the last remaining clouds of dust are thinning, and I see a line of ships taking shape in the haze. Four lean ships take form: destroyers, with their pennants numbers flying proudly from their yards, and battle-ensigns at their mastheads as they steam in stately procession through the gate into Grand Harbour.

'What is it?' I ask a three-badged killick.

'That's the *Sikh*,' he says with a catch in his voice, 'and behind her comes the *Maori*, the *Legion*, and a Dutch destroyer called the *Isaac Sweers*. They have sunk two Itie cruisers; the *Da Barbiano* and the *Di Giussano*, off Cape Bon.'

'How do you know that?' asks Laura.

He grins knowingly. 'How do the Malts know anything? The word just gets about. Look at them!' He waves an arm and we follow his finger as he points. A wave of sound begins to swell. There are black dots swarming along the tops of the walls, and coloured groups waving from every vantage point as the four ships slide down the harbour. Their crews line the upper-decks and their sirens whoop triumphantly as they are greeted by the deeper blare of merchantmen. The tugs join in with toots of their own, and the growing volume of cheering fills the sky.

Laura pulls herself tight against me. 'I think I'm going to cry,' she says, and she is not alone, for there are tears everywhere as we watch them sail in.

'You comin', chief?' the killick is asking. 'I think the cox'n is eager to get away before the next raid.'

I look at him and nod. 'Yeah, I'm coming.' I turn to her for a second, and she presses the small jeweller's box into my hand. 'You must give this back, Ben. It is too expensive for me to hold on to.' She reaches up on tiptoe and pecks me on my cheek.

I go down into the pinnace. The cheering has died now. The people just staring in quiet groups as the destroyers seek out their berths. The pinnace shoves off, and I stare back towards the shore, to see several women praying in the background, but mostly I see a neat figure in a Wren's uniform.

Nine

To suggest that anyone is glad to be back at sea would be absurd, but there is a general air of relief in the boat as we leave astern the oppressive squalor of the island and dive to put distance between it and us before we surface for the night. It feels as though we are deserting a sinking ship as Malta slips away. Already *Tarantula* is on full alert, for there are reports of U-boats lurking in the area, waiting to pick off strays like us as we leave the swept channel. However, today we see and hear nothing as the motors push us away from the land, and darkness moves in to cloak the world up top.

There is not a young face in the boat now. Even those who are young in years have a mature, knowing look about them when they take over their familiar duties in a quiet, professional manner. There is no form of training that could ever achieve this. It requires a baptism of being under attack and staring death in the face; of knowing that they may never see another sunrise or feel another wind. It turns them into veterans. They have been there and back, and any hoary old salt who takes them to one side in a dockside pub and tries to spin them a yarn will choke into silence when he sees them staring back at him with knowing eyes that have seen it all.

In the familiar, fetid atmosphere the same backsides slide into the same indentations on the same seats. The controls fit easily into their hands, although *Tarantula* is too new to have acquired the worn, palmatal grooves of her elder sisters. There is a noisy game of nap taking place in the fore-ends, with cards slapping down hard on the table, and piles of cash in front of each player, for there has been little to spend money on and the betting is heavy. If this was a cruiser or a destroyer I would put a stop to it at once, but in a submarine moving out for another patrol it would be flying in the face of tradition, and they do not even attempt to hide the money away when I come prowling along on my usual tour following a spell in harbour.

'Did you get a good run ashore, Swain?' asks a torpedoman. 'Clump reckons 'e dipped 'is wick in Floriana.'

'Like 'ell 'e did!' snarls a two-badged seaman. 'Yer can't get near to a Maltese party. Even the whores 'ave it padlocked these days. If yer do latch on to a decent party the whole bloody family chaperone you, twenty-four hours a day.'

'That's all you know,' grins Clump, lifting his eyes from an Egyptian AFO*. 'A bit of nutty and a chunk of 'pusser's 'ard' soap got me a knee-trembler. Didn't even 'ave ter ask 'er ter pull 'er pants dahn either, cos she was wearing pusser's underwear.'

'Dirty young sod!' sniffs the two-badgeman, 'it'll drop orf before yer starts drawin' yer tot. Didn't yer daddy give yer nuffin ter play wiv when you was little?'

'Course 'e did – my little sister.'

'When I gets out of this mob I'm gonna buy a car and shag me way round the country, jest to make up for all I've missed,' yearns a falsetto voice.

'Yer wants a motorbike fer that,' asserts Clump.

'What the hell can yer do on a motorbike?' yells a chorus.

'Yer puts 'er arse on the saddle and 'er shoulders on the 'andle-bars. Then yer puts 'er feet in the footrests, starts the engine, and yer can shag at sixty miles an hour orl the way up the Great Norf Road.' One of his own boots whistles past his head as the compartment explodes with laughter.

Satisfied, I turn to make my way aft again, and notice Jumbo sitting like a big evil gnome in an isolated corner, scowling out at us. 'Why don't you keep that stupid mouth of yours shut for a change?' he growls in a voice loud enough to quell the laughter and sober us all. The big second coxswain looks huge and aggressive as he stares at us with his face twisted into a look of contempt. 'If you can't talk sense you should keep that trap of yours shut,' he repeats.

The card game goes silent and Clump stands with his mouth opening and closing. I move over to stand looking down at

* Egyptian Admiralty Fleet Order – Illegal pornographic book.

Jumbo. 'Bit jumpy today aren't you?'

He glares up with his eyes ablaze. 'I don't see anything to laugh at in that filth. These bastards seem to 'ave short memories. Well, I haven't. I don't forget that easy, and I wonder if we are fightin' a war or just tryin' to win medals for some people.' He makes no attempt to hold down his voice, and there is an air of embarrassment in the fore-ends.

'You've got things twisted, Jumbo,' I tell him with a heavy warning in my tone. 'I'd keep those ideas to yourself if I was you.'

He stretches up to tower over me. 'Are you tryin' to tell us that we are not out to make a name for the skipper?' he sneers. 'It don't take much in the way of brains to work out that 'e's bin on the carpet for exceedin' 'is orders. I don't mind skippers who take chances, but this bloke's suicidal!'

This is dangerous talk, both for him and the boat. Somehow I must take the steam out of the situation without too much fuss. 'If you've got a gripe you can come and see me about it quietly; not broadcast it through the boat. You should know better than that.'

'If you mean that I should come sniffin' round your backside like some bloody OD you can forget it. You might fool some of these simple sods, but I'm no zombie. What are you gonna do about it, Swain – slap me in bloody irons?'

'What's going on, Cox'n?' Falstaff's even voice comes from behind me. He is looking from Jumbo's belligerent features to mine. 'We can hear you in the wardroom.'

'Fine!' snaps the second coxswain insolently. 'That's just what I wanted.'

'Keep your mouth shut!' I yell at him.

I can see sweat breaking out on his face and realise that he is having a hard time controlling himself. Falstaff must see it too, and we both recognise what lies beneath the outburst. It is Jumbo's way of saying he has been pushed too far and I must nip it in the bud.

'We will decide what to do with you when we reach Alexandria, Moore,' warns the first lieutenant. 'Your behaviour between now and then will determine what happens. In the meantime, for your sake as well as your messmates keep your misguided thoughts to yourself. Is that perfectly clear?'

Jumbo breathes heavily, sucking in deep breaths as he tries to control his emotion, while the rest of the lads try to look anywhere but at us. *Tarantula* sings quietly, as though she is listening to what goes on. We will never know what effect Falstaff's words have, for at that moment the klaxon screeches; eating into the tension like an axe, and we get caught up in the wild rush to diving stations.

It is purely routine, but Martingale wanted to make certain that we are on our toes, and I bless him for it. We are about to go up for the night, to charge the batteries and change the air. The skipper is at the forward periscope, making a final search before committing us to the surface. He cannot have failed to hear part of what went on in the fore-ends, but he doesn't so much as glance at Jumbo when the big man slumps into his seat beside me. We hold her level at thirty-two feet while Martingale takes his time scanning the shadows. At last he is satisfied and snaps up the handles with a nod towards the leading stoker on the raise-and-lower lever. The long shaft slithers down into its well with a silky sound, and there is not so much as a tear from the new flange.

'Surface!' he orders briefly, and launches his body onto the ladder. The needles sweep round the dials and we feel the first roll as she hits the swells, then the hatch thumps and orders come down the voicepipe, the diesels rumble, clean air fills the control room, and she climbs a long swell before thumping over to plunge deep into the next one with a sound like half a ton of gravel hitting the hull. It is as if *Tarantula* breathes a sigh of relief as the orders come to go into 'patrol routine', and I prepare to serve out the rum. There is something comforting in the steady rumble of the engines and the even swoop of the hull as she plunges along. The rum burns my throat with a pleasant glow as we settle to our first supper at sea. The talk is quiet and unabrasive as we try to forget what took place in the fore-ends just half an hour ago.

Martingale chooses this quiet moment to tell us where we are bound, and why. He paints an elaborate picture of events taking place in the eastern Mediterranean. It resembles a gigantic chess game played by two invisible antagonists whose moves must only be guessed at. It involves important pieces which have to be moved and protected with stealth and precision. There is bluff and counter-bluff as each side strives to out-think the other, and *Tarantula* is just one of the pawns in the complicated pattern.

The British are determined to get a supply ship through to Malta from Alex. They choose a veteran whose name will become synonymous with the island's struggle against starvation and defeat. HMS *Breconshire* is a naval supply ship, carrying five thousand tons of precious cargo. She is due to sail from Alex with a vast escort of two cruisers, an anti-aircraft cruiser and eight destroyers. Four more destroyers and another two cruisers will reinforce them as she moves westward, until a whole battle-fleet is employed to see her through.

At the same time the Italians are answering a call from the Axis forces in North Africa for supplies of fuel and ammunition by sending ships from various ports along routes that will take them through the Strait of Messina, down the Adriatic, and along the coast of Greece, to rendezvous somewhere to the west of Crete, before splitting up to make their runs to Tripoli and Benghazi. Air reconnaissance reports say that there are heavy units of the Italian fleet at sea to the north of us.

The two opposing forces are converging on each other along the legs of a big 'L'. No one can predict where they will meet, and although it concerns us in the overall pattern of events we will remain aloof and go about our own affairs, which involve following up the information gained from those documents and the diary Jumbo and Falstaff discovered in the half-submerged schooner.

We know that the Decima Flotilla is planning a raid, and that the submarine *Scire* is involved. We also know that the attack will take place before Christmas Day. The facts have been analysed by the experts and they have come up with their own theories, but no one is going to stick out his neck and guess at where the Italians will strike. Martingale's ploy to get past Boxwell must have gone astray, because the fat captain's signature appears on our orders. I wonder how Laura will come out of it now that her bosses have clubbed together to ensure that Martingale is kept in his place.

His voice has a strange, pensive quality as he continues his spiel. 'I have talked the situation through with the other officers, and we have ruled out the western Mediterranean as a possible target. The only base is Gibraltar and although an aircraft carrier would make Il Duce's mouth drool, the Germans are hogging that end.' He takes a moment before going on. 'Therefore, we can assume that the attack will come somewhere east of Malta. Possibly along the North African or the Palestine coast; between Tobruk and Haifa. We have narrowed it down to Alexandria.'

His voice drops a little, as though he is letting us into a secret. 'That is a bit further east of our patrol area between Sidi Barrani and Mersa Matruh, so I have sent off a signal asking to have it extended, for I want to take *Tarantula* within shouting distance of the port in an attempt to ambush the Italian boat.'

He takes a breath before going on. He sounds tired, as though he is weary of butting his head against a brick wall. 'All the training we did in Scotland could bear fruit now. I am going to presume that we will get permission to patrol the new area and push on in that direction. We must be on our toes even more than usual as we approach the zone, but I know I don't need to remind you of that. Just keep your fingers crossed that I have guessed right.'

We all know the odds against coming anywhere near to that Itie submarine, and I cannot help thinking that if permission does come, and Boxwell's signature is on it, there will be some hidden motive behind it. Perhaps hoping that this time Martingale will hang himself when he comes up empty-handed. Somehow though, I have an illogical trust in our skipper. I really do believe that he can find that small boat in this vast ocean, even though it sounds crazy. It is one reason why I am still carrying the little jeweller's box about in my pocket, waiting for the right moment to give it back to him. Something tells me that there never will be a right moment, and that I will still be carrying the bloody thing when we reach harbour. Maybe then I can give it to him without disturbing his judgement.

'Cox'n to the bridge!' The shout comes from the control room and drags me from the mess and up through the gale of wind blasting down the conning-tower to find Martingale and four lookouts up top. This should have been the navigator's watch, so I assume he has been allowed below to make up his charts for the new course, while the skipper handles the boat.

'Sir?'

He twists around in the deep gloom and stares at me for a moment. 'If I didn't know you better, Grant, I would think that you were hiding something from me.'

'I have been sorting out my stores, sir,' I mumble, thankful that he has turned away again so that I can get a grip and hide the guilt on my face.

He focuses his binoculars on the darkness ahead. 'I see. Are they okay?'

'Yes, sir. I could have done with more salt, but it's scarce in Malta.'

He looks into my face again. My eyes are becoming used to the darkness now and I can see him studying me thoughtfully. 'I must say, I never expected you to keep secrets from me,' he accuses. 'It seems that I am to be featherbedded by both my first lieutenant and my cox'n.'

'There is nothing amiss, sir,' I explain, much relieved that he and I were on different tacks. 'Nothing that we can't sort out without the need to bother you. Domestic stuff. We didn't want to bother you with the sordid details.'

He grins knowingly. 'All in the best submarine tradition, eh? I won't blame you for that. I know enough about you both to realise that I will be put in the picture at the right time. To use one of the first lieutenant's favourite lines, my friends are poor, but honest.'

I remain silent as he stares back into the empty night. Clouds are rolling in from the west like sheep on an inverted moorland. The wind moans a melancholy dirge through the periscope standards and *Tarantula* curtsies to another swell. It is a wild and beautiful night, with a cold, black, undulating desert spreading out in all directions. The war seems a million miles away at this moment.

'That brings me to another issue,' he goes on quietly. 'You delivered my package?'

'Yes, sir.'

'You saw Laura?'

'Yes, sir.'

He turns to me again. 'You are not being very forthcoming, Grant. You must know I am hungry for news. You were ashore a lot longer than I would have expected, so I assume that you had plenty of time to get my message across.'

'I got caught up in a couple of raids, sir. We had to take shelter, and everything came to a stop when those destroyers came into harbour.'

'We?'

I could bite my stupid tongue. 'Laura and I, sir.' I look straight into his eyes. 'She had time off so we went and sat together in a small bar and talked a bit.'

He stares back at me; waiting. 'Well?'

'Er – it's a tiny bar tucked in under the cliff, as good as a proper air-raid shelter, and run by an ex-bootneck. It is where they all go for breaks from the ops room.'

His eyes are searching mine. 'You're still telling me nothing, Grant.'

'Sod it!' I'm thinking. 'There's no way out now.' I take a deep breath. 'She took the box and opened it, then asked me to take it back to you, sir. Here it is.' I reach into my pocket, knowing that I have made a real cock-up of things, but I can think of no other way to tell him. 'She said that she'd no right to accept it from you, sir. That you assume too much, and that she is not thinking of getting married.' I get a grip on myself and take the plunge. 'In fact, she is not in love with you, sir.'

He flicks the case open to stare down at the brooch for a moment. Even in the dim light the silver sparkles and looks even more beautiful in the cold indigo of night. 'You must have had quite a long intimate chat with her.'

I decide to go the whole hog. 'When the second raid came we went to a small house she rents, and drank cups of tea while the enemy knocked hell out of the harbour. We chatted between the bangs.'

'I'll bet you did!'

I look straight at him. 'Seems that we both got it wrong, sir. It's me she loves, not you.'

His mouth drops open. 'Well, I'll be jiggered! You are a dark horse, Grant!'

'Sorry, sir,' I say lamely, somewhat puzzled by the way he is reacting. If I had been expecting fireworks I couldn't have been more wrong. He is not ranting and raving, or tearing his hair out. I know he isn't the type to fall apart, but I did expect some show of disappointment.

'Oh, don't apologise,' he says pleasantly, still looking at me with incredulous eyes. 'It was a fair fight for God's sake! Well, well, well, who would have thought it? Pipped at the post by my own cox'n.'

'I – I held on to the brooch because I didn't want to upset you, sir.'

His grin widens. 'She has found herself a good man, Grant. Here!' He hands me the jeweller's box. 'Take this with my blessing, and give it to the lady when we get to Alex, because I know she will be there waiting when we arrive.' He leans closer. 'Maybe there is a wedding in the offing?'

I splutter. 'We – we – er – haven't got that far, sir.' I cannot keep the bewilderment from my voice. It is as of he is discussing a prize filly for which he has been outbid, and I feel a cold anger welling up inside me. Somehow his off-hand acceptance cheapens the whole thing in my eyes.

'If you don't pull your finger out and marry the girl I shall demote you to AB,' he jibes. 'You will deserve no better.' He changes tack. 'Poor old Grant; you must have gone through the mill trying to sort out a way of telling me.'

I am beginning to boil now. 'You did mention something about getting married to her yourself, sir. It would seem logical that you would be upset.'

'That's right,' he says casually, 'and I do think it is about time I began to think of settling down, and who better to do it with than Laura. However, if I cannot have her, there is no one better than yourself. No hard feelings at all, I promise you.' He turns to concentrate on the swirling night while I try to choke back my pique.

'Bridge!' the voicepipe calls.

'Go ahead!' he responds, and because my ear is almost as close to the mouthpiece as his I hear every word of the helmsman's report. 'Sub-Lieutenant Telford says he has decoded a signal, sir. It is urgent and immediate.'

'Very good! I will come below. Ask the navigator to come up and relieve me.'

When he is gone I am left alone with my thoughts for a moment, fingering the small box and wondering if it is all a front with him, and all that couldn't care less attitude is merely a bluff. After all, how could he react any other way and not lose face? And no captain must do that in front of a rating, least of all his own coxswain. I raise my binoculars and peer ahead into the bluster to find the sea as confused as my thoughts. Maybe I have maligned him. Perhaps deep down he is hurt as I would expect him to be, but there is no way that he can reveal it. *Tarantula* is smashing her way along as though she knows there is something big ahead, and the navigator finds me a dull working partner for the remainder of his watch.

When I go below at the end of the watch I find there has been a change of plans. We are on a new course that will take us north-east to an area between Cape Matapan and Crete. Fleet Air Arm planes have reported seeing a submarine on the surface heading towards the gap north of Suda Bay, and we are trying to head her off. Looking at Martingale as he bends over the chart I can see that he is brooding over the new orders. All throughout the long day he hardly utters a word, and we learn to steer clear of him unless it is absolutely unavoidable. I know that it has nothing to do with our discussion on the bridge. It is the new orders that he is unhappy about, and he stalks the control room all through the day and well into the night while the diesels drive us on towards our new patch.

Wednesday the seventeenth finds us creeping into position, with the loom of Antikithera Island off the starboard beam as he makes one all-round sweep before diving the boat.

Hour after hour we patrol up and down this unfriendly place, where enemies watch from every vantage point. We are always conscious of the clear sky and try to ignore the fact that any keen-eyed airman can see our dark shape at forty feet, so that when we are forced down we have to swim blindly up to periscope depth, knowing that they could be waiting for us.

In case we miss the enemy boat three Hunt class destroyers are on patrol to the east of the island. They are spread out in a long line just to the south of Karpathos, and at times like this we realise just how vast the ocean is to a dived submarine whose limited vision is restricted to what may be seen from a periscope lens that is no more than a foot or so above sea-level. The enemy has it much easier with his lofty headlands, aircraft, and whatever sophisticated detection gear he has installed on those coasts. His ocean must seem a lot smaller than ours.

The whole of that day we sweat it out, on edge all the time, and Martingale hardly saying a word or leaving the control room. Several times we are forced to go deep when aircraft or ships come nosing along. Then comes that nervous climb back to thirty-two feet, listening for every sound, and knowing that we will not hear a waiting aircraft, or a suspicious warship lying hove-to with engines stopped, while her operators listen to our screws bringing us up through the opaque depths to within range of their depth-charges.

When we surface we receive yet another signal with a change of orders. It is now assumed that the U–boat has left our area and we are to join the search to the south and west of Crete. In one way it is a blessing, for now we have much more sea-room, and those three friendly destroyers are not too far away. There is plenty of depth too: over a thousand fathoms beneath the keel. Six thousand feet and more stretching down into the dark caverns where weird creatures play, through pressures that could crush *Tarantula* like an eggshell if she slips down too far. We are suspended in this three dimensional world where the natives are much more colourful and far better adapted than we to cope with the environment.

It doesn't do to dwell on it too much. Everywhere we go; up or down, port or starboard, there is danger, and we must remain alert to it without allowing our imaginations to run riot. Small wonder that submariners become a special breed. They are more like the living organs of a submerged leviathan than a ship's company, for they make her breathe, give her movement, and carry her stink with them wherever they go.

Our engineers do us proud tonight. They push her hard, so that by morning they have taken us one hundred and sixty miles eastward to a well-defined area that verges on that of the patrolling destroyers. It is extremely important that we remain in our patch, for they are nervous and touchy; poised ready to attack anything that moves on or below the surface in their sector. In some ways they are more vulnerable than we are, for they have nowhere to hide when the bombers come, or a couple of big Italian cruisers home in on them. We neither see nor hear them, but we can sense their presence just over the horizon as we help them to search for the elusive shrimp that could be anywhere between Rhodes and Mersa Matruh; if she exists at all, and is not just a figment of some over-keen airman's imagination.

Sometimes however, we are allowed a miracle, and providence steps in just when we are about to despair. When we prepare to surface after yet another fruitless night we pick up the distant thump of a depth-charge, followed by a pattern of eight, each clanking against the hull like someone trying to attract our attention by hitting our skin with a metal rod. Much against our natural instincts we swim off in their direction as fast as we can go.

Martingale is clutching at straws. Hoping that those are our depth-charges, and that whoever is dropping them is not chasing shadows. We pile on speed, and even before full darkness comes he takes us up without so much as a cursory glance to make certain it is safe; broaching while a blood-red sun still soaks the sky and turns the ocean dark olive while we spread our sparkling wake half a mile astern. Once again he is ignoring orders to remain in our own area and using every ounce of power to drive us to where the action is. As though she senses his impatience *Tarantula* leaps along with her bow-wave high above the casing and her exhausts hurling great sprays of black-tinted water into the sky. The signalman is up top with the skipper, ready with his Aldis, and the challenge and response firmly fixed in his brain as we race along at seventeen knots. Every cup and saucer, knife and fork, loose metal lid and bucket handle jingles to the vibration as the engineers open the throttles wide.

We spot them long before they see our low profile, and Bunts triggers our challenge at the dark, circling shapes cutting into the horizon. Immediately we get the correct response, and we begin to breathe easy again. They are not over-pleased to see us, however. 'Stand well clear!' signals the lead destroyer curtly. 'We are attacking a firm contact.'

We sheer off, staying at full speed while we make a wide sweep. We must assume that the U–boat is much too busy trying to evade her attackers to know about us. We know only too well what she is going through, and how blind she is as she plunges from depth to depth in her efforts to fool her persecutors. She will be deaf too, for her ears are numbed by the charges and the beat of propellers. She will not hear the meagre sound we make as we circle, watching the professional way the destroyers go about their business. These are no novices, nor are they greedy, for they share their expertise, with one, or sometimes two of them lying off to pin-point the target while their mates go in for an attack. Even from this distance the sound of charges hit the hull like a sledgehammer.

Martingale stops both engines and creeps along slowly on one motor so that Trump can train his hydrophones to listen to what goes on below. There must be a whole mess of confused noise for him to decipher. The racing screws of the destroyers, the disturbed water, and overpowering all, the detonations of the charges. Too much to allow any distinct sounds to be identified, yet he must listen in case she slips the net and comes in our direction. She may be on the run, but she is lethal. We can even feel a twinge of sympathy for her crew, because we have been there too, but it lasts for only a second, for although they live in the same environment it doesn't make them fellow creatures.

For two hours the pounding continues, until it seems impossible that they have not crushed the life out of her. We lose count of the number of charges or their attacking runs. Sometimes they all stop to listen, and Trump concentrates hard from the sideline. The range is too great for our hydrophones to identify individual sounds, for they are more than three miles away, and we can only guess at what she is doing.

How can they miss her? She has nowhere to hide? Yet she keeps wriggling off the hook. If they don't get her before morning her mates will turn up to chase us away. How long has she been down there? How much air has she left inside her pressure-hull? More importantly, what is the state of her company, now that they have been subjected to hours of sustained punishment? They will hear the stealthy sound of asdic fingering the hull, and cringe in anticipation as the churning screws go over the top, holding on tight to control their nerves in that infinite moment before the detonations come.

Trump reports propellers speeding up again, and we can see their shadowy shapes moving in to attack again. Two this time.

Two dark shapes crossing the path of the moon as they home in on the U–boat. Trump drags his earphones away as the explosions come. There is a period of quiet while they circle their quarry. Suddenly a light starts to blink at us, and Bunts clacks his response. 'They can smell oil, sir,' he reads. 'They have sounds of blowing on their hydrophones.'

A distant whoop of triumph drifts down on the wind and we watch a finger of brightness leap out from a destroyer to probe the water. They are gloating over the mess that bubbles up to the surface. When Martingale passes the news down into the boat no one is in the mood to cheer.

'The wolves have preyed; and look, the gentle day!' Falstaff has come to stand behind us and watch the circling ships. Sure enough, the rim of the world is edged with the silver of a new dawn.

Martingale's voice is icy cold as he tell Bunts to call up the destroyer and ask if the 'kill' is confirmed.

The Aldis clacks again. 'Come and see for yourself,' Bunts dictates solemnly.

Through the leaden sea we creep in on our motors, for Martingale insists on maintaining listening watch. The destroyers take shape now as they cut into the lightening sky, their lean, hungry silhouettes prowling about the scene, and we can already smell the sickly stench ourselves as we draw nearer, and it smells like the stink of a decaying corpse. In other circumstances we would make such a stink, and it is enough to turn my guts. There is flotsam dotted about too, spreading like a burst boil across the scummy water. Not much to mark the grave of fifty-odd human beings.

Martingale takes us right up to the edge of it, despite the protesting blinks of one outraged destroyer that has to swing clear when we push past as though they don't exist. When I look at him his eyes are narrowed as they stare down into the patch of filth that is staining the ocean. 'Stop both!' he orders quietly, and the way drops off until we drift through the outer edge of the mess. The destroyers prowl like jackals, but he ignores them completely.

'They are asking us to stand clear, sir,' warns Bunts.

'There is no blood and guts amongst that lot,' states Martingale, as though he has not heard.

One of the destroyers has ranged alongside, and I can see helmetted figures staring at us from her bridge. A loud-hailer crackles into life and a resentful, metallic voice shouts, 'I would be obliged if you would haul off. This one belongs to us!'

We are so close now that we have no need for a hailer. 'I am not convinced, sir,' yells Martingale through cupped hands.

There is a stony silence from the other ship for a moment or two, and we drift even closer together. You can almost sense their outrage from here. Once again the speaker bellows. 'We have five buckets full of assorted rubbish, including items of clothing. What more do you want – blood?'

That is precisely what he does want; hopefully with a few choice pieces of entrails to go with it. Real, tangible, multi-coloured proof that carnage has taken place here. The destroyers have searched and hunted long and hard. Their captains are all senior to Martingale, and they have no intention of having the wind taken out of their sails by an impertinent submarine skipper. The angry voice comes back. 'I am satisfied that we can claim a kill, and can see no point in risking my ships on a needless search for proof.'

Martingale goes to the voicepipe. 'Trump! Have you heard any more noises from below?' He must have got a negative reply for he cups his hands again. 'Sir! Two things make me think that it is worth further investigation. There are no signs of her crew, and we have heard no breaking-up noises.'

This time the voice has a sardonic edge to it. 'Then you stay here and search at your own risk. I will not endanger my ships watching over you.' With that the three ships squat their backsides into a welter of foam and go speeding off like indignant tarts.

'Clear the bridge! Stand by to dive!'

Five minutes later we are ninety feet, with Trump training his electronic ear full circle to listen for a phantom sound that only the skipper really believes will come. While he leans across the HSD's shoulder Falstaff moves out of earshot, and Jumbo turns to me. 'I see we are gonna play silly buggers again. What makes him think he has a monopoly on brains?'

'Keep silence and attend to your job!' I snarl as Falstaff darts a suspicious glance in our direction.

'Stop both!'

Now is the testing time for Falstaff's trim, for without the aid of the hydroplanes *Tarantula* hangs suspended over a thousand fathoms of ocean while everyone stays perfectly still and silent. It is as though every seam and rivet is part of a huge sound-board, waiting to catch the faintest whimper of noise. We will never know what inner voice convinces Martingale that the U-boat is still alive, and, in all honesty, very few of us are with him on this one as the long minutes drag by for almost a quarter of an hour before Trump's harsh whisper runs through our bodies like an electrical charge. 'I can hear her, sir.'

It is the most unprofessional report that I have heard him make. And from one who is always so pragmatic it comes like a thunderclap, dragging every available eye in his direction. 'I can hear sounds, but they are impossible to identify.'

'Here!' Martingale grabs at the earphones and clamps them to his own skull. I have nothing to do while the boat hangs dead in the water, so I watch his face as he concentrates. His mouth twists into a cruel smile. 'That's her all right, and she is in bad trouble. She is running her pumps and judging from the other noises, she is having problems with her shafts. I'd say she is a very sick boat indeed.' He hands back the 'phones. 'What do you make of it?'

Trump listens with his expert ears. 'Sounds pretty desperate, sir. She bleedin air into her tanks now, and I can hear a grinding sound, as though she has a warped shaft.'

'Or two,' confirms Martingale with satisfaction. He straightens to look at Falstaff. 'She is badly wounded, but by no means dead; not by a long chalk. I reckon that she must have found a layer of high density to sit on, and now she believes the destroyers have gone and she is on her own. She is struggling like mad to get up top, and I doubt if she can hear us at all. If she is a German boat she will have the GHG group-listening gear – *Gruppenhorchgerät* they call it. In perfect conditions it can pick up a single screw at about twenty kilometres. Not today though, my crippled friend, not today.'

'She must know that Crete is just beyond the horizon, and she must be short of air, sir,' suggests Falstaff.

'Yes,' agrees Martingale, 'but I doubt if this skipper is another Rahmlow. He will be a veteran if he is German, or he would never have got through the Straits into the Med. He will have instincts just like me, and he would not be blowing air and making all that noise if he was not desperate. If his damaged boat allowed he would creep up slowly before committing himself. Right now he is having the devil's own job controlling her, but if he is an old hand, he can still be dangerous.' He licks his lips as though he is anticipating a feast. 'We will play it his way. I will not go up until he is about to surface. If we time it right we will have him dead to rights.'

'One torpedo will finish him off,' gloats Falstaff.

The skipper looks at him with a half-smile. 'No. Number One. We have been handed this one on a plate. We are going to make a present of this boat to all those doubting Johnnies back at base.'

Falstaff's face is deadly serious. 'I must remind you that we are within a short flying distance of enemy air bases, sir. There is only one way that we can hope to get that boat to Alex – on the surface; probably on tow – right through Bomb Alley.'

'Nothing ventured, as they say,' declares Martingale firmly.

Ten

While Trump listens to the struggles of the crippled U-boat Martingale spells out the way we are going to tackle the job. Speed and surprise are the essential ingredients, for she must not be given time to get a signal off to her mates in Crete and bring the Luftwaffe howling out to gum up the works. It will be up to the gunlayer to get his first round off before she recovers from the shock of seeing a strange submarine pop up within half a mile of her, with all tubes loaded and aimed straight at her belly. A couple of bursts from the Lewis-guns should emphasize that we are in no mood for compromise when Martingale calls on her skipper to surrender, and tells him that any attempt to abandon or scuttle will be considered an act of aggression. We will open fire immediately with guns and torpedoes, and not waste time looking for survivors.

'I mean that,' he stresses in a hard voice. 'That will be the crucial part of the operation, for if they see a chink of weakness on our part they will try to scuttle their boat. Unless my instructions are followed to the letter there will be no survivors. That is the only weapon we have. Her commander has to choose between surrendering his boat and killing his own crew.'

He takes a moment to allow that to sink in, then goes on, 'If this is a standard German U-boat there will be four containers just forward of the gun, with rubber rafts for the crew. If they behave themselves they will be allowed to use them to paddle away: In weather like this they have no real problems reaching safety. We shall take her captain and one other officer home for the intelligence boys. That's all.'

He replaces the microphone and turns to Falstaff. 'There is one change to the drill, Number One. I will be in command of the boarding party, which will consist of the cox'n, second cox'n, two ABs, Chief ERA Billings, EA Roper, and two stokers. If all goes to plan I shall send most of them back, along with the prisoners.' His tone becomes even more serious. 'This is the most important bit as far as you are concerned. If we are attacked you must slip the tow and get below without hesitation. Whatever occurs *Tarantula* comes first. Any heroics on your part and I'll have you court-martialled if we survive. Understand?'

Falstaff nods. 'Yes, sir. It is a bit unorthodox for the captain to go on one of these jaunts though, isn't it?'

'This is an unorthodox affair altogether. I would get all the volunteers I needed if I called for them, but this is my gamble, and if necessary I will remain behind on my own once the tow is secured. Your only real concern is for *Tarantula* and her company.'

'That tow is my job, sir,' objects Jumbo from his seat. 'I am the second coxswain.'

'You will do as you are bloody well told!' roars Martingale, glaring at the big man. 'This isn't a tea-party, and you have already made your feelings plain, do you really think I can trust you alone with me?'

Before the embarrassed man can reply Trump calls urgently from the Asdic. 'She is having problems, sir. Not finding it easy to get to the surface.'

Martingale takes the earphones. 'You're right. They are running the pumps like blazes, and just listen to those shafts; it sounds as though they're lubricated with sand. Ah!' He gasps, with a sudden lift in his voice. 'She is blowing everything by the sound of it.' He hands back the earphones. 'Keep an eye on those bearing, Trump. We must keep the bow pointed straight at her.'

He takes one last look round at us. 'All right, let's get on with it. Everyone to his station. Remember, Guns, I am depending on you to get your first round away in record time.'

'Aye aye, sir!' The gunlayer is already moving into the wardroom to open his lower hatch. His number two follows with a round of 4-inch, semi-armour-piercing shell cradled in his arms. No need to worry about those men; they are professionals with gun-drill etched into their brains.

I take a deep breath to quell the flutterings in my belly. It is all in the lap of the gods now. If that boat is Italian, the odds are that her skipper will be rational enough to know when he is beaten. If she is a German U–boat with another Rahmlow in command his reaction could be much the same. Somehow, however, I have a feeling that this bloke is one of the other kind: One of the 'do or die for the Führer' variety. He held out against three destroyers who should have had him for breakfast and are even now congratulating themselves on a kill. They had him by the short hairs and he wriggled off the line. We will need to watch this joker every second.

'She's coming up, sir!' Trump's urgent voice drives all those trepidations away. I straighten up and grip the hydroplane wheel with tight fingers. Behind me boots clank up the conning-tower ladder. I can visualise the skipper and the gun-layer hunched up against their upper hatches, waiting for Falstaff's whistle.

'Broaching now, sir!'

'Surface!'

I spin the hydroplanes to 'hard rise' as air blasts into the tanks. At twenty feet Falstaff blows his whistle and both hatches jump back into their latches as a deluge of water hits the deck beneath the tower. Guns is on top form today, for the first round thuds in my ears even as I leap out of my seat to join the rush. We break all the rules as a crowd of rampaging men swarms up top before the boat has time to settle onto an even keel. The harsh rattle of the port Lewis shatters my eardrums as I emerge from the hatch. Bunts is firing a stream of shells laced with red tracer in a low arc across the U–boat as she wallows drunkenly with her stern awash. She looks desperate, and I can see that she is one of the classic Vllc German ocean-going boats with a bandstand on the after end of her bridge. She is ugly and mean, and we will never have a better opportunity to plant a torpedo where it will do most good, and deep-down I wish that was what Martingale intended to do, for I have a strange foreboding inside me that warns that this time we are taking on too much.

There are heads popping up cautiously above the rim of her small bridge to peer over at us, and this time both Lewises pump away, sending them groping for the deck. The 4-inch fires again as Guns keeps up a steady barrage.

'Cease fire!' yells Martingale above the racket, and as the guns go quiet he gives a succession of orders to bring *Tarantula* round in a tight circle, taking us well clear of the U–boat's after tubes and opening up a view of her big eighty-eight. Anyone who is stupid enough to try to man her weapons won't know what hit him.

There is an officer wearing the white cap of a U–boat skipper lifting his head above the rail as the lull in the firing continues. He has another officer at his side, and they hold their hands high as they see *Tarantula*'s bulbous bow staring back at them with all eight tubes aimed at a spot right beneath their feet. Martingale picks up his megaphone. 'Do you speak English?'

The one with the black cap waves an arm and yells back through an old-fashioned voice trumpet. 'Yes!'

We are within twenty five yards of her, with our bowdoors wide open. One flick of Tod's fingers could blow her out of the water. 'Bring your men up from below one at a time. Tell them to go forward and line up on the fore-casing, well clear of the gun,' orders Martingale, dictating his words slowly so that there can be no mistake. 'Remember, I know how many men make up your crew, and one false move will bring an immediate response. If I suspect that you are trying to scuttle your boat I will have no mercy. I shall sink you, and I have no intention of picking up survivors – is that understood?'

The officer waves a hand and consults his commander. 'We agree,' he calls back, 'but we are hardly afloat; even though we are using the pumps!' His English is good, clipped, educated stuff.

'Get your men up now!'

They come piling up from below, blinking in the sunshine before climbing down over the bandstand and working their way forward past the gun to form up on the casing, looking like a row of black crows on a washing-line. The men on our guns watch narrow-eyed. One move to release the traverse lock on the eighty-eight will bring wholesale slaughter, and the Germans know it.

'Leave that!' A man jerks upright as Martingale's shout comes like a gunshot to stop him opening a life-raft container. 'I will tell you when.' His warning is emphasized by the officer, and they all stare across at us with malevolent eyes.

'Now,' he continues. 'Stand by. I am bringing a boarding-party over.'

'We are having difficulty staying afloat!' repeats the officer anxiously, and judging by his skipper's angry reaction he does so without obtaining permission.

'Good!' I think to myself, 'the more nervous bastards amongst that lot the better.'

'Bring up the dinghy!'

It is done in record time, for no one wants the fore-hatch open for one second longer than absolutely necessary. The inflatable is one of two we use to land secret agents, and this is the first time either of them have seen daylight since they came on board.

'First lieutenant to the bridge!'

Falstaff must have been hovering close to the foot of the ladder, for he appears like magic before the skipper is finished speaking. The rest of us are already on our way down to the casing, where Jumbo and his mates are launching the dinghy. We have to do the crossing in two goes because even at a pinch it will hold no more than four men; hence the choice of eight to make up the boarding party.

The skipper, Jumbo, Clump and I go first, to take charge of the U–boat's bridge and cover the crowd on the fore-casing with our sten-guns. We take a line across with us so that the dinghy can be hauled back and forth like a ferry. It will be much easier than paddling and leave the hands free when we pass the towing hawser across.

Boarding is easy. All we have to do is run up onto the after casing where it is well awash and scramble out. The casing is much wider than ours, and has a slatted-wood deck, from which it is a simple matter of climbing up to the bandstand to face the two German officers waiting on the bridge. The English-speaking one peers anxiously at us from behind his skipper, but it is the master who holds our attention. The last time I saw an expression like that was on a fishmonger's marble slab. It is the colour of parchment, with bloodless lips and eyebrows so fair that they are hardly visible. Deep lines run from his sharp nose to the edge of his mouth, and his eyes are set in deep sockets. He looks cold, arrogant and cruel.

The junior officer steps forward to introduce his skipper. 'Kapitänleutna—'

'Not now!' snaps Martingale rudely, holding up a hand. 'We have no time for that. When my engineer arrives we will go down together to inspect the boat.' He holds his revolver aimed straight at the Nazi skipper's belly. 'Tell your captain to behave himself, for my men and I are extremely nervous.'

By now the other four members of the team have reached the U–boat and are climbing on board. When they are all assembled Martingale orders the German captain to lead the way below, then turns to me. 'You, the second coxswain and Perry remain up top and guard the men on the casing.'

They disappear through the hatch, leaving us to survey the motley bunch. Some are squatting down on the damp casing, while other prefer to remain standing with their heads bent. No one utters a word, and all the while *Tarantula* wallows lazily in the oily swell with her big, gaping tubes staring at us like the eyes of an owl.

The minutes tick by slowly. If I glance over at the other bridge I can see the faces of Falstaff and his bridge-party quite clearly as he uses the motors to hold her bows-on. A cold December sun shines from out of a cloudless blue sky. The U–boat has a sickening feel to her that shows how unstable she is, and I wonder once more if all this effort is not going to be wasted.

Any further contemplation is interrupted when I hear voices filtering up from below. Unlike *Tarantula* this boat has a large conning-tower beneath the upper-hatch with enough room for several men to squeeze in to man the push-button controls of the helm and the attack periscope. In fact it is a sort of attack centre, with firing levers just above the helmsman's head. The air-search periscope is down in the control room.

The German skipper leads the way up, looking twice as sulky as he did before as Martingale prods his stern with the revolver. 'You can tell your men to unship their rafts now,' he orders. 'Take things quietly, and when they are inflated, hold them alongside until I tell you to start boarding.'

'But there are only four, and each one only holds five persons!' protests the junior officer.

'Too bad!' Martingale eyes him coldly. 'They will have to take turns on the rafts while the rest use their lifejackets and hang on to the life-lines. There is not far to go.'

The yellow inflatables are nothing to write home about. They expand into big, soft bladders as the air-bottles feed air into them. Even when they are fully inflated they are not as rigid as our own black ones and lollop about on the surface like seaside airbeds. 'Rather them than me,' I think to myself as I watch them scramble aboard. It is quite a fiasco too, for everyone seems to have his own private method of doing it; ranging from a tentative one-foot-at-time, approach which seems to always end up with a ducking, to a full-blown leap that threatens disaster and brings shouts of outrage from those already there.

It is amazing just how many bods can squeeze onto a raft when they really try, and some bright spark has remembered two additional rafts that are stowed beneath the casing. So, although they look very uncomfortable, most find a place, and now it depends on the vagaries of wind and tide to get them to dry land. From my point of view it is a relief to see them go.

It is not the end of our troubles by a long chalk, for the U-boat is in a much worse condition than we feared, and far from sending back most of our men, Martingale has to retain everyone and ask for another ERA and stoker PO to help run the pumps and try to stop up some of the leaks. Most of the water is coming in at the stern, but it would be pointless to try and shut the after compartment off, because she will not float with it flooded. Luckily the batteries are situated forward of the bulkhead, so we do not have to worry about chlorine gas for a while.

We have a couple of volunteer Germans down below. A thin-faced engineer and one of his mates who seem as anxious as we are to keep their boat from sinking. The Nazi skipper is ferried across to *Tarantula* when the dinghy makes its journey to fetch the extra men and the towing-hawser. I'm not sorry to see the back of him, with his steely eyes and silent hate. The English-speaking officer seems to have accepted the situation and remains with us; in fact, there seems little love lost between him and his boss.

By mid-morning the tow is secure, and the U–boat is no further down by the stern, so maybe we are winning. Falstaff takes up the slack and slowly builds up speed until we are racing along at about one and a half knots. He intends to increase until we are keeping up a steady three knots, and no one needs to be a genius to work out that it will take us more than four days to reach Alex if we cannot get help with the tow.

It is a dismal thought. Not even the wildest optimist believes that we have a cat's chance in hell of surviving all that time on the surface with no escort. So we code up a signal, break radio silence, and scream for help, praying that no sharp-eared detector is picking up our transmissions. I get a brief, sadistic satisfaction when I think of the Hunt class destroyer's captain reading our message, but it is short-lived when I consider that those three ships are most likely our closest allies.

Miraculously the horizon stays blank all through the day, and we get an added bonus when one of the U–boat's diesels starts up and settles to a nice comforting rumble. Any idea of using it to push us along is dispelled immediately we engage the clutch, for the shaft produces an unearthly scream and glows red-hot after a few minutes. Nevertheless, it keeps the batteries charged and draws in a cool breeze to make life more bearable to those who are sweating below.

Apart from the twisted shaft and the various waterfalls our main problem is a big gland which is below water level, and needs to be tightened up on to its seating. The ERA swears that it has been loosened and unseated deliberately, and when I think back to that look on the German captain's face I can well believe it.

There are numerous other leaks throughout the boat which could be contained by the pumps, but until we get that gland tightened the water is gaining. Any responsible insurance company would accept that she is a write-off and pay the money, but not Martingale. He listens to a long list of defects, orders the rudder locked amidships, then turns to with the rest of us, making her as seaworthy as possible for the long tow home.

On the bridge we cast longing looks towards the horizon

in the hope that we will see three destroyers appearing over the rim before the enemy arrives. For some reason it takes until mid-afternoon before we get a reply to our signal, and when it is decoded we wonder why they bothered to answer at all, for it promises nothing.

'Maybe they're sulking,' someone sneers.

We organise watches and use the bunks in the officers' quarters just forward of the control room bulkhead, where the atmosphere is less cosy than *Tarantula*'s wardroom, but still better than we are used to in the chiefs' mess. The Germans seem to go out of their way to make their boats spartan, and that central passageway must lead to congestion when everyone is trying to get to his diving station. There is plenty of good grub on board though, and it isn't long before we have a meal organised. It is all becoming nice and cosy, and I sense a certain optimism creeping in, until I look at Jumbo's surly face. He has become possessive about his towline, as though he thinks he is saving the boat on his own, and remains below only for as long as it takes to eat his grub.

During the middle watch another signal comes to tell that a tug is on its way out to us with an escort, and that we can expect some air-cover tomorrow. At last they are becoming alive to our predicament, but it seems that our three friendly destroyers have other priorities, and we have to sweat it out for yet another full day before that tug can hope to reach us.

Our hopes begin to fade when there is still no sign of a friendly aircraft by noon, and we begin to feel very neglected again. To add to our troubles the weather has decided to take a turn for the worse. It would not have been unwelcome if it had brought a touch of bad visibility with it, but as often happens, the moment there is a hint of rain in the atmosphere, you can see for bloody miles.

The tow becomes more difficult as the U–boat yaws and stretches the hawser to breaking point with showers of spray springing from the taut strands as it sings a warning song. Reluctantly Falstaff drops the revolutions until we are barely making way, and our hearts slump with them. We know how hard it is to locate a submarine in the middle of an ocean, but few of us have a kind word to say for the RAF as the southern sky remains blank. As if that was not enough the stern gland leaks like a basket when the stern goes deep and the water-level rises in spite of the pumps.

Martingale and the German officer are on the bridge with me when the tow finally parts. We are virtually hove-to when *Tarantula*'s stern goes one way and the U–boat bow goes the other, with the inevitable result. Once she breaks free the U–boat performs a wild dance of her own to make life even more miserable for the men cramped up in the stern. It is impossible to hold our feet as she hurls herself about, and Jumbo's men have to crawl through deluges of spray to save themselves from being swept overboard. They come onto the bridge like drowned rats, and all we can do now is watch hopelessly as Falstaff makes a slow circle; then Chief ERA Billings comes up to say that we are losing the battle with the stern-gland, and the after-ends are flooding.

'All we need do is stick it out until the tug arrives,' persists Martingale. 'The odds are that she will have extra pumps on board. Can't you hold out until then?'

'No, sir,' states the ERA bluntly.

'What if we were to trim down forward to lift the stern?'

Billings shakes his head slowly. 'It won't work, sir. All that would do is hurry the end. We have drained every tank we can, and it is still not nearly enough.'

Martingale ponders hard for a moment, then swings on the German officer. 'Can we get rid of some extra weight?'

The officer shakes his head. 'We have already dropped the ballast keel, and most of the stores are forward. By the time we have got out any significant amount it will be too late.'

'What about the stern torpedo tube?'

The eyes light up for a moment. 'It is loaded.'

'Well, that's one and a half tons we don't need,' says Martingale eagerly, 'let's get rid of it.'

The light goes out of the German's eyes and he shakes his head again. 'First you must flood the tube and open the outer door. That might be too much.'

The ERA looks from one to the other and shrugs. 'I honestly do not know. The further we dip the stern the more pressure there is on the gland.'

'We won't achieve anything just standing here,' snaps Martingale. 'Have we any torpedomen on board, Grant?'

'Clump, sir – I mean Perry.'

'Send him down below.' He turns to the German. 'Care to give it a go?'

'*Ja*. I will come with you. I have the knowledge to fire it!'

They drop down through the hatch, with Clump's number elevens clattering down after them. We are having to hold on tightly now as she bucks and weaves all over the place. Perhaps it is my imagination, but it seems to me that every dip she makes leaves a bit more of the casing awash. In my mind's eye I see Martingale and his small party cramped into that minute area right aft with the sound of water sloshing about while the pump struggles at full power to keep down the tide. They will be opening up the valves to admit more water to flood up the tube round the sleeping torpedo, then the outer door will swing open to the sea. Martingale will nod at the German officer to pull the firing-lever, and a charge of compressed air will drive out the torpedo. I look aft towards the stern as it corkscrews just beneath the surface. I feel a slight jolt when the tube fires. Her automatic-inboard-vent system is not working correctly, for I see a big bubble burst just aft of the duck's-arse. No matter, for we have no need to hide the tell-tale bubble today.

Now they can shut the outer door and drain down the tube. I realise that I have been holding my breath and keeping my fingers crossed since I saw the bubble. The water has crept right up past the after aerial support to reach a pair of bollards situated a third of the way along the after casing. What is more the bow is not rising to compensate, so that the whole bloody boat slumps deeper and deeper; despite getting rid of a ton and a half of torpedo.

I look at the angry sea. It is not going to be a simple matter dragging the dinghy through that lot, but if we start now, before the weather deteriorates even more, we might manage. When Martingale comes back to the bridge he must see how she has settled and give the order to abandon.

How wrong can I be? He watches *Tarantula* come round on one of her long sweeps and waits until she is abreast, within hailing distance, before he shouts over to tell Falstaff that we are holding our own, and there is still time to get another tow secured. The dinghy will not be manned, however. It will be used to take the weight of a manilla rope to haul over the heavy hawser. The skipper reckons that once we get her under way there will be less pressure on the stern gland, which should help the pump to cope. He doesn't convince me, and by the looks on their faces, the others are not sold on the idea. Least of all Jumbo. He is looking down at the casing where he and his lads are expected to work waist-deep in water while large waves wash over them. They will require one hand for themselves and one for the hawser as they haul it in inch by inch. He'll need every ounce of his strength to take the brunt of the work when they try to shackle the eye onto the cable once more.

'Right,' says Martingale. 'You remain in charge up top, while I go below with the engineers to see what else can be done to keep her afloat. Let me know when the tow is secured.'

'Sir!'

'Well?' he asks impatiently.

'Should I let you know if the stern goes under any more. You won't notice anything while you are right aft.'

'I have no intention of drowning, if that's what you mean, Grant. Believe me, I shall know if things become desperate.'

'Aye aye, sir,' I reply glumly.

He looks into my face and relents a little. 'Just keep an eye on things, and don't panic,' he urges quietly, then ducks below and leaves me watching the antics of Jumbo and his men as they risk life and limb with that bloody hawser. From time to time they disappear altogether under a welter of foam when she ducks her stern, but always they re-emerge spluttering and gasping, to haul in another couple of feet. Falstaff is showing his talent for ship-handling as he manoeuvres *Tarantula*'s stern as close as he dares. For one horrible moment I hold my breath when it seems her rudder must come crashing down on the U–boat's bow when he allows her to come too close. It hovers above Jumbo's blokes for a long moment before soaring even further skyward and swooping over to one side. That is enough to scare the living daylights out of me, but now it looks as if he has the message, for she keeps her distance.

Jumbo is a tower of strength as he heaves his huge body about in the turmoil. He spends much of his time hanging on to his men when they flounder and fight to stay on the slippery deck, and it is mainly through his efforts that eventually I can cross my arms above my head to tell Falstaff that we have the tow secured. They struggle aft hand over hand as the sea tries to rip them off the casing, until they reach the bandstand and climb up to slump exhausted onto the deck.

'I'll watch the tow,' I tell them. 'Get below and have a rest for a while.'

With one accord they look from the submerged stern to my face and shake their heads. 'Not bloody likely, Swain,' growls Jumbo. 'It's a generous offer, but I think we'll stay up top, if you don't mind.'

'Suit yourselves,' I snort, though I don't really blame them. There is no doubt in my mind that she is getting lower and lower, and when *Tarantula* manages to drag the bow upwind the only difference is that her antics become less wild. I look at the sky and find it glowering back at me. It might hide us from aircraft, but it promises no good at all when it comes to staying afloat. Big swells are sweeping the whole length of the boat with ominous regularity. Surely they must hear it in the after-ends?

I keep looking at the hatch, hoping to see heads appear when Martingale finally admits defeat, but it gapes back vacantly as she lurches and judders with the tow stretching bar-taut. It spells disaster, and I doubt whether even Martingale believes we will survive until the tug arrives. In the end I can bear it no longer. 'Watch things up top,' I order Jumbo. 'I am going below.'

The motion and noise is much more frightening down here. The long, dank tunnel is claustrophobic, and the thump of heavy seas breaking over the casing above my head is continuous. Right aft in their small cavern they look like demons as they work thigh-deep in black, scummy water. Billings is bent double as he manipulates a large spanner in an attempt to tighten a submerged nut, while the others tend to his needs and follow his instructions. They are trying to re-seat the flange after stuffing in some make-shift packing, and when they notice me hovering in the gloom they glare at me as though I am intruding in their tiny, oily world. Martingale's voice is angry when he barks, 'I thought I told you to stay up top, Grant!'

'The casing is well awash, sir,' I insist, staring into his wild eyes. 'She can't hold out much longer, and the weather is getting worse.'

'Get back up top and let me do the worrying,' he snarls. 'We have located the source of the leak. Once we have it under control the pumps will keep her afloat. So you can go up and tell the others to keep a look-out for the tug and keep the tow secure.'

I glance round at the sallow, stubborn faces and decide that they are all as mad as the skipper. British and German alike, looking at me with grim determination. I back off slowly, then turn and make my way forward with a lump in my gullet. Maybe they will succeed. If he does pull it off Martingale will have put one over on Boxwell and his circle of doubting croneys, yet somehow I think that is a side issue now. The real purpose is to get this bastard home against all odds. Who would have thought a time would come when enemy seamen could work together to save a lousy chunk of scrap? I heave my body up through the conning-tower while she throws me against the sides with her vicious whiplash movements. There is a strange new feeling inside me when I look at Jumbo and his men slumped into their corners with water streaming from their clothes. I meet the second coxswain's eyes and find the same belligerence burning there. I wonder what turns submariners into a separate breed; whether it takes a certain type to volunteer, or do we become moulded by a long tradition?

There's Clump sitting splaylegged, with his big boots in everyone's way. He is nobody's idea of a hero, yet he was down there with Jumbo just now, clinging for dear life while he wrestled with that vicious serpent of a hawser. In that sophisticated world ashore they would not give him house-room, yet blokes like him are worth their weight in gold when the boat is in a jam. I lean on the rim of the bridge to look out towards *Tarantula*'s bouncing stern. There are pale faces staring aft from her bridge, and even at this distance I sense their concern. They are our shipmates, and what we are feeling goes way above any patriotic ideals.

I shake off these thoughts and come back to reality as another wave bursts with an explosion of white against the fore-part of the bridge. The heavy clouds rolling across the sky in cumbrous procession look so low I feel I could reach up and touch them. The shadows of another night begin to take over, and unbelievably, we have survived the day. That tug will have thumped her way a hundred miles nearer, and if I was a praying man I would be offering up thanks right now.

A sudden commotion from the hatch makes me swing in time to see the head and shoulders of the German officer emerging. He is closely followed by others, until all except Martingale and Billings are up top. I turn to the stoker PO, and he looks back at me with hopeless eyes. 'He sent us up out of it.'

'Why?'

He shrugs. 'That gland is not going back as it should. As fast as they tighten one side it opens on the other. If anything it is worse now than when we started. We tried to shut the bulkhead door so that we could build up some pressure inside the compartment, but the bulkhead is warped. In any case, there is so much water in her now, nothing we can do will save her. She is a gonner, Swain.'

'How long have we got?'

The German officer breaks in. 'There is no telling.' He speaks in his own language to one of the engineers, then looks back at me. 'An hour at the very most.'

'What's the skipper doing?'

'Dunno,' says the PO. 'Him and the chief are working on something, but we were told to get out.'

'I'm going down,' I grate determinedly. 'You had better call *Tarantula* and tell the first lieutenant what's happened. We must get off her before it is too late. Is that a signal lamp?' I ask the German.

He lifts the trigger-lamp from its socket on the side of the bridge. '*Ja*.'

'Anyone know any morse?'

'I do,' states Jumbo. 'I've got enough to get a message across.'

'Well get on with it, we haven't much time.' I scramble down through the hatch and go stumbling aft towards the persistent rumble of that single diesel.

The bulkhead door to the engine room swings loose as I go through, and I see that the water is lapping over the lip of the sill. The bloody place must be half full by now! I drag my reluctant body past the hammering rockers towards the two hunched shapes in the tapering confines of the stern. They are working up to their armpits in the polluted foulness as they grapple with the flange.

'It is time to get up top, sir!' I shout above the racket of the diesel and the storm beating against the hull.

Martingale's eyes blaze at me. 'Get out! I ordered you to remain on the bridge!'

'There's no point to this any longer, sir,' I persist. 'You have done all that you can. The German officer says that we can last only a few more minutes!'

For a second I think he is about to lash out at me. His face is contorted and his eyes wild. Then he chokes back his rage with an effort. 'I won't say this again, Grant. Get up top! I'll come when I am good and ready.'

I look at Billings, still reaching down with his spanner, but staring back over his shoulder. He looks ill with exhaustion, and doesn't seem certain of what is going on. 'What about him?' I ask Martingale. 'Are you going to sacrifice him too?'

'Give that spanner to me!' he yells at the startled engineer, and snatches the tool from his hand. 'Now – up top, both of you!'

For a moment the chief hesitates with his white eyes flickering from one face to the other, but I have no more time to waste and grab at his sleeve to haul him bodily after me. 'Come on, Billings. There is room for only one silly bugger down here.' I push him ahead of me and turn for one final go at Martingale. 'I don't know what you are trying to prove, sir, but I do know it is bloody useless. You can have my chief's rate if you like, but I'm telling you straight that you are acting like an idiot!'

To my surprise the anger dies and his face breaks into a wide, white-toothed grin. 'I am touched at your concern, Grant. I won't hold this against you when we get ashore. Five minutes is all I need to tighten this last damned nut, then I'll know that I have done everything possible to save her. In spite of what you say, I still believe she can last until that tug gets here.'

As though in response the U–boat gives a sickening lurch, and I sprawl across the compartment so that our faces come close together. He doesn't look insane, and maybe he knows something we don't, so I refrain from smashing my fist into his jaw and taking him out by force. 'All right, sir, I am getting the men off as quickly as possible.'

'Very well. So long as the tow holds I see no reason why we should not take precautions. We can slip the hawser from *Tarantula*'s end if necessary.'

'There's no future in hanging about down here, sir.'

'We'll see. Get on with what you have to do, and allow me to continue down here.' He starts to turn away, but hesitates to look into my eyes. 'Good luck, Grant.'

I choke back a lump. 'Same to you, sir.' I wait just long enough to see him bend back into the sludge.

Falstaff and Jumbo have organised a ferry and the men are going across in pairs. Passing the tow-line through their hands as eager mates haul them through the turbulence. It is a wild, dangerous business, and they work in silence while I glance down anxiously into the gaping mouth of the hatch. Finally only Jumbo and I are left standing there.

'You had better go,' I tell him.

He looks at the water swirling up round the bridge. There is no doubt at all that she has only moments to live. Each succeeding wave swamps the bridge and pours a few more gallons into the hull. 'What about the skipper?' he asks.

'I'll go back for him. I will drag the stubborn sod up by the scruff of his neck if I have to.'

He passes the line from the raft to me. ''Ere. 'ang on to this. I'm bigger than you.' Before I can put up an argument he drops through the hatch and is gone. I raise my head to see a light blinking from *Tarantula* and look about for ours. It is a single-handed affair, so I blink a hasty 'Stand by!' and leave them to sort it out, for I need to concentrate on that hatch.

Suddenly the U–boat gives a lurch to end all lurches and I know she is going down. I let go of the line and drop my feet over the rim of the hatch, then feel myself lifted clear by the sea as she hoists her bow into the sky and begins to slide from under me. I splash about, trying to find the hatch with my clutching fingers. I can feel her sucking at me, but my lifejacket is holding me up. Something snakes across my shoulders and I grab at it instinctively. The line goes taut and bites into my wrist. I feel myself being dragged through the water until I come up hard against the ballast-tanks, and strong hands are hauling me up as *Tarantula* picks up speed to take her away from the whirlpool that marks the spot where the U-boat went down. I stare at the disturbance until the sea closes in and wipes out all the signs.

I am being led to the bridge where Falstaff waits. My head is whirling and my body is a mass of aches and pains, but I hold back from going below. We look at each other and I try to say something, but the words won't come. He places a hand on my shoulder. 'The purple testament of bleeding war,' he says in a choked voice.

Eleven

Alexandria lifts out of a milky haze as though the houses and trees are planted in the ocean, for the city is built at sea-level. Fort Qaitbay, Fort El-Ada and the Raz El-Tin Palace make good marks for the navigator when he takes bearings to fix our position: Not that he really needs to bother, because we are met by two smart patrol-boats who take station ahead and astern to escort *Tarantula* in through the boom. No sooner are we through than a cutter hauls alongside, and a lieutenant leaps aboard to come up to the bridge with an air of some excitement, as a signal-lamp from shore spells out a message, telling us to heave-to near the entrance.

'I have brought you this,' states the lieutenant, handing a black bundle to Falstaff, who shakes it out to display a skull-and-crossbones, with a couple of symbols. 'What the hell is that for?' he asks angrily.

The lieutenant is not much more than a youth and his college-boy exuberance glows on his well-scrubbed face. 'You are to be cheered in, sir.'

'Cheered in?'

The youngster becomes a little agitated under the steady gaze of half a dozen bearded scruffs. His face grows more serious, and there is something in his tone and manner that suggests that he is not quite so adolescent as he looks. 'Yes, sir. You see, we need something to cheer about in Alex right now. Last Friday morning some Italian human torpedoes got inside the harbour to sink *Queen Elizabeth* and *Valiant*, then went on to blow the stern off the Royal Fleet Auxiliary tanker *Sagona*. You will see the two battleships sitting on the sea-bed when you clear the headland. That was just eleven days after we lost *Prince of Wales* and *Repulse* in the Far East, and less than a month since dear old *Barham* went down. Everyone is feeling pretty sick about it, and we need a booster for morale.'

'You know that we have lost our captain and second coxswain?' Falstaff asks harshly.

The youngster draws himself upright. 'Yes, sir. We do know that. Nonetheless, you have fought a battle and come off best. You and your ship's company deserve the accolade that goes with it. A communiqué has been circulated throughout the fleet, and with your permission I will read what it says.'

'Go ahead,' says Falstaff drily.

The lieutenant pulls out a document. 'It is headed "Back From The Dead", and goes on to say, 'After being trapped on the sea-bed by several enemy ships, His Majesty's Submarine *Tarantula* rose like a behemoth to retaliate. The enemy found that her bite was as venomous as that of her name-sake as she scattered a convoy and sank an ammunition ship, before making a dramatic escape through minefields. Not satisfied with that, the submarine then went on to track down and capture a German U–boat, and only severe storms prevented her from bringing her prize back to Alexandria. Regretfully, her commanding officer, Lieutenant-Commander Martingale, and his second coxswain died in their herioc attempts to keep the damaged U–boat afloat.' He looks up, slightly embarrassed. 'There's more of course, that is the relevant part. I – er – hope you don't find it too colourful.'

'You wrote that?'

He smiles whimsically. 'It is part of my job.'

'Dressed it up somewhat, didn't you?' sniffs Falstaff.

'That is part of my job too,' he admits defensively. 'But the basic truths are there, and only the timing has been condensed a bit to make it look as though the events ran in sequence on a short patrol. It is a piece of blatant propaganda if you like, but right now we have not got a single operational battleship in the eastern Med, and there is a certain amount of panicky reaction taking hold in the port. Some of the ships even keep their screws turning to discourage further frogman attacks, and there has been a number of false alarms. We have to stabilise things, and *Tarantula* fits the bill nicely.' He looks into Falstaff's hostile eyes. 'It is no more than you deserve, sir, and it will give a fillip to a despondent fleet. I am sure that your captain would not grudge his ship's company their moment of glory.'

Falstaff turns aside to look out at the sombre ships moored in their open ranks across the pool. He nods grudgingly. 'All right; let's get on with it.'

The lieutenant hesitates. 'Ah, well, we would like you to wait until ten-thirty before making your entrance. The ships are going to "clear lower decks" and muster Marine bands to play you in.'

'Good God!'

The youngster bristles. 'If it is to be done at all, it should be done well, sir.'

Falstaff sighs and looks down at his watch. 'Nearly two hours to wait. What do you suggest that we do, just circle about aimlessly?'

The lieutenant brightens. 'We have thought of that, sir. You may secure alongside the small RFA tender over there. That will keep you hidden in the 'wings', so to speak, until it is time to make your grand entrance.' He grins disarmingly. 'It is all in a good cause, sir.'

The day is hot and the flank of the tender cuts off any breeze that might have kept the hull cool, and the boat from oozing condensation. Everyone who is not required below will line up on the casing when the time comes, and there is a desperate search going on for respectable clothing to wear for the occasion, but however we try, we are still going to look a pretty unwholesome lot; unshaven, unkempt, and uninterested. When I mention this to the lieutenant just before he takes his leave he grins at me. 'That is all to the good, Chief. The more piratical you look, the more effective it will be.'

He waits for two belted and gaitered seamen to escort our Nazi prisoner into the cutter, then snaps a salute at Falstaff before dropping into the sternsheets. I watch the cutter sweep away towards the anchorage. I have always had an aversion to pen-pushing parasites who prey on other people's misfortunes to make their living, but there is something about this bloke that I can't help liking. He has embellished the truth, but someone had to do it, and somehow his motives have an honest feel to them.

Tarantula sits and sweats while we try to tidy her up for the big occasion. The seven-man crew of the tender do their best to make things pleasant for us by providing fresh bread, fruit and vegetables. Her skipper and mate are a pair of hard-nosed, hard-drinking seamen who would have got Falstaff and the other officers blind drunk given half a chance, but their offer is politely declined.

I have no scruples when I accept a large tot of whisky from the disappointed mate as he comes to stand with me on the casing. 'We can do with something like your submarine to boost things up,' he declares as we take alternate swigs at the flask. 'The army seems to be doin' all right in the desert now, but old Rommel got to within a couple of hundred miles of Alex at one stage. The Gyppos were practising how to say 'you jig-a-jig my sister' in German and Italian.'

He finds me poor company and a waste of good whisky, so eventually goes off muttering something about 'bible-punching tee-totallers'. I am not surprised, for I have a dead feeling inside that refuses to be shifted, and when I go through the boat I find it reflected in the faces of most senior ratings; although the likes of Clump and his croneys are looking forward with lewd anticipation to visiting the less salubrious quarters of the city. 'You come back with a dose, and I'll keep you on stoppage of leave until your balls drop off,' I warn him.

'Don't worry, Swain,' he grins. 'I won't get more'n a nap 'and'. Nuffin that the quacks can't cure wiv a dose of M an' B, and a few number nines.' He leers at me. 'There is none so pure as the purified, yer know.'

I force a smile. Nothing I can say will deter him and his mates from over-indulging. I can only hope that they stay off the native hootch and at least come back with something that is curable. I go up top again, where I find Bunts preparing to hoist our new 'Jolly Roger' on the after periscope. We find out later that this is a sort of tradition here, and the flag is presented whenever a boat comes in after blooding herself on her first kill. Someone has made a fine job of it, and beside the skull and crossbones there are two white bars; one with a 'U' cutting through it to denote a submarine. We have a long way to go before we match *Torbay*'s record of sinking two merchantmen, six sailing vessels and an Italian submarine in the space of a week, but we happen to be in the right place at the right time to receive an official pat on the back, and it will do no harm to the crew's morale after losing the skipper.

There is almost a surge of pre-performance nerves when the

moment draws near for us to slip our moorings. Some of the men are like excited schoolboys when they line up on the casing, tallest for'ard – shortest aft. We are going to miss Jumbo's lofty figure at the front today. He was easily the tallest man of them all, and now the symmetry is lost as his stocky understudy takes his place at the head of the line.

Falstaff uses the electric motors to take us away from the tender and down through the lines of ships. *Tarantula* cuts the sparkling surface like a knife, moving quietly and easily, as though she is loath to disturb the water, and our two faithful escorts bring up the rear to turn it into a small procession. Above my head the black flag snaps a couple of times then wraps itself round the periscope, and stolidly refuses to open out again to display our emblems. The men stand with their legs braced and their hands clasped behind their backs. I can see now that the lieutenant was right; they do look more impressive with their two-week-old beards and shabby clothes.

I see nothing herioc in their appearance, just a kind of sad dependability that goes with the job. They spring to attention smartly enough when Subby snaps an order in response to the trill of a bos'n's call from a passing ship, or the brassy blare of a Marine bugle from one of the cruisers. There are a few chests swelling when they see the lines of white-clad sailors manning the upper-decks, and hear the controlled cheering as caps are raised in unison. The military music is hard to distinguish from this distance, for all we can hear is the deep rasp of tubas and the steady thump of drums, but Bunts is hissing 'Hearts of Oak' through his teeth, so I assume that is what they are playing.

Now the depotship comes into view, lying stern-to the crooked pier that eats into the harbour from the seafront. There is a small U–class boat already secured alongside, but we are ordered to tie-up starboard-side-to with the busy coast-road close to port. Falstaff is at his best today and makes a fine job of going alongside. We would not have cracked an egg as we sidle gently into place and the heaving-lines go snaking across. The extra bodies break ranks and leave the work to the casing party as they double-up the hawsers and ropes and get the plank out ready for Falstaff to be first one up the long ladder to the big ship's upper deck.

The cheering parties have dismissed and gone back to their

normal duties. I cannot help wondering if all this has had any real effect at all as I go into the motion of getting the boat into harbour routine, and the men start to carry their gear inboard. They are looking forward eagerly to hot baths and oil-free clothes. The hatches are opened to allow the diesels to suck the stale air out of the boat as they charge the batteries. There is always a sort of holiday atmosphere when we secure and open up the boat, and I see the men relishing the feel of the sun on their backs and the breeze on their faces.

I wish that I could share their pleasure, but I find myself reluctant to follow them inboard, and long after my mates have gone I sit in the mess, staring into space with a head full of sombre thoughts. I don't even know what is really bothering me. I thought I had come to terms with Martingale's death: we all lose mates from time to time, and learn to take it as a matter of course; even though it hurts for a while. I can even accept the showy ostentation of our entrance as part of the game, yet I have this sick feeling in the pit of my belly that will not go away.

Eventually I have to go up into the depotship with the rest, to scrub the grime from my body and relish the feel of clean clothes. This should be a moment to savour, and I have my tot to look forward to in a few moments. I can relax without the slightest niggle of fear, so I should feel on top of the world, but all I have is an empty, dead sensation.

There is a film show that evening on the depotship's well-deck. A James Stewart thriller that is right up my alley, but after sitting through the first half hour of it I begin to feel stifled and have to get up from my seat and seek out an isolated spot in one corner of the upper deck. It is a deep purple night, full of gunmetal shadows and a multitude of stars, more numerous and larger than I have ever seen before. The sky stretches away towards the desert like a vast plain beyond the silhouettes of buildings. There is a magical quality to it that draws out a man's thoughts and sends his mind down strange paths. Somehow tomorrow I must stop acting like a wet-eared OD and come to terms with being a coxswain. In two days time our new skipper arrives, for Falstaff is going back to the UK to do his 'perisher' before taking up a command of his own. We have to get used to a new skipper and 'jimmy the one', and it is part of my duty to bridge the gap between the 'troops' and their new masters, for we need to bring *Tarantula* back to full working order as quickly as possible.

Standing here on my own I can begin to get things back into focus. There is a fresh feel to the wind as it comes in across the Sahara with the dusty smell of dry sand in its breath. Even from this short distance the chaotic noise of the city is muted and I can hear the black water lapping against the hull. At last I begin to sense a new resolution welling up inside, and this all-prevailing calmness is allowing my brain to function along the right lines. Somewhere out there in the desert blokes are being maimed and killed, and so long as we can prevent Rommel's supplies from getting through the loss of blokes like Martingale and Jumbo has a value. The few boats we have out here are overstretched and war-weary, but so long as we keep Malta hanging on like a thorn in the enemy's side we are doing our job. It is not just patriotic verve that makes me itch to get back into the arena again; it is a genuine desire to help those squaddies in the desert, and make Martingale's death worthwhile.

I push myself away from the guardrail and clank down a steel ladder to the maindeck. There is only one place for me with these thoughts running through my head, and I feel the need to take one more foray through the boat before I turn in. I make my way aft, but my mind must be still in a whirl, for I take the wrong ladder that leads to the starboard passage instead of the one on *Tarantula*'s side, and because the film show is still in progress I have to go right aft to the quarterdeck before I can cross over to the other side.

There is a leading seaman doing quartermaster's duty near the after gangway, with a young bos'n's mate standing beside him. They are tucked in under the overhang of a gun sponson while the officer of the watch stands near the rail with his telescope under his arm. I salute the quarterdeck and ask permission to cross the sacred area.

The quartermaster is in a friendly mood. 'Okay, Chief,' he says cheerily. 'You will find that on this ship submariners come first in everything.'

I know that he means what he says, for this old lady is well-respected in submarine circles. She is far removed from her 'pusser-bound' counterparts who seem to consider boats as a bit of a bloody nuisance at times, and go out of their way to ensure that a little service discipline is instilled into the scruffy reprobates who climb wearily inboard after a hard patrol. She knows how to treat her brood, and if you mention her name to anyone who has enjoyed her welcoming comforts you will get a knowing smile. We know that she is a 'one-off', and that some incompetent bastard made a complete balls-up when he produced this depot-ship, for she functions too well, and gives priority to all things submersible, and we know that we shall never see her like again if we ever lose her.

The quartermaster is a comforting man to talk to: one of that special breed of time-serving veterans with a solid, professional way of looking at things. He is what I need at this moment; someone who is completely unbiased, who knows nothing of the things that went on in that U–boat. It does me the world of good just listening to him explaining in his quiet, simple way, what happened on the morning when those Italian frogmen entered to blow holes in our battlewagons as they lay inside the heavily defended harbour.

He grins a devilish grin as his mind goes back to the panic that ensued after the attack. 'Runnin' rahn like 'eadless chickens they was. A couple of the frogmen surfaced and swam to a mooring buoy, and I reckon every rifle in the fleet took a shot at them. Dunno which one went up first, but it was 'alfway through the morning watch when the explosions shook the place rigid. Christ, you should 'ave seen the flap! I reckon every winder in Alex rattled with the bangs, and when it calmed dahn a bit I could see both battlewagons sittin' on their arses in the mud.'

We have wandered across to the guardrail as he talks, and I look down at *Tarantula*'s lean shape nudging against the catamarans, feeling new life pouring back into me. Her trot sentry has strolled right up to the bow to stand and stare longingly at the town, and I recognise him as one of the stokers. They must have completed the charge early, and in the traditional manner of submariners, both engineroom brigade and seamen have got together to share the stints on the casing. I doubt if anyone has to do more than an hour on guard-duty tonight.

It is time to go, but as I turn to say goodnight I freeze. There is a familiar, portly figure standing in the centre of the quarter-deck, and I sense the quartermaster's anxious look when I gasp and take a step towards it. The noise must have attracted his attention, for Boxwell swings to look straight at me. I can see the recognition in his face before he deliberately turns away to stroll over to the stern.

I take a second involuntary step and a hand bars my way. 'What do you think you're doin', Chief?'

'That's Captain Boxwell!' I blurt out stupidly.

'That's right,' he agrees cautiously, still holding on firmly. 'You still can't approach an officer wivaht permission though. You should know that, Chief.'

'What's going on?' asks the officer of the watch, striding towards us.

'That's Captain Boxwell,' I repeat inanely, without taking my eyes away from the pompous shape. 'I have to see him!'

The hand gets more persistent and the officer plants himself squarely in front of me. 'Don't make things difficult, Chief.' There is an ominous warning in his voice.

My mind works fast. 'I have to see him, sir. I have a message from my captain.'

He looks suspicious. 'I heard that your captain is dead.'

'Yes, sir,' I flounder about as I try to think. 'Yes, sir, but he was engaged to one of Captain Boxwell's secretaries and I was supposed to deliver a message if I could find her.' I pull out the jeweller's box. 'I was supposed to give her this. Captain Boxwell must know where I can find her.'

'Wait here.' He nods at the quartermaster before striding off towards Boxwell, who has been joined by another officer to stand in deep conversation. When the officer of the watch interrupts there is a short altercation and faces turn to look in my direction before Boxwell shakes his head. The officer returns with his features set hard. 'He will not see you now,' he says bluntly.

'Take it easy, Chief,' warns the quartermaster when he feels me tense up. 'Don't do anythin' you'll regret.' I look into his sober, anxious face. He would understand if I told him that Boxwell and his crowd could have warned of the impending attack if they had not been so determined to squash Martingale, but no-one else will listen, and it is too late now.

'Okay,' I say, pushing aside his arm. 'I will go through proper channels in the morning.'

He nods and drops his arm down to his side. The officer backs off a bit as I glance over to where Boxwell and his companion have resumed 'walking the deck'. There is nothing to be gained here, but if I play it by the book I might find out Laura's whereabouts, and I suddenly need to do that more than anything in the world.

With my mind in order once more I decide to leave it for now and tackle Falstaff in the morning. With luck he will still have time to get me an audience with the illustrious captain, or at least find out what I want to know himself. When I stretch out in my hammock under the soft-breathing ventilation shafts I search back in my mind for pictures of that time in Malta and realise part of what is eating at my insides. I can hardly contain my impatience as I try to sleep in this unfamiliar environment, without the smell of diesel or the sea washing over the rounded hull close to my right ear.

In spite of being in a hurry to tie things up before he flies off for his Commanding Officer's Course, Falstaff is only too willing to do what he can for me. He knows part of what went on between the skipper and Laura, and that I was involved somewhere down the line. So he goes clattering up the long ladder in search of Boxwell immediately after the hands turn to for work. I try to get on with my normal duties while waiting for him to return, but I become more impatient as the morning drifts by until tot time before he puts in an appearance.

'Bad news I'm afraid, Grant,' he says. 'It has taken me ages to locate the elusive captain, and when I did it was only to find out that he has flown back to Blighty to take up a new appointment.' He sees the look on my face and grows concerned. 'I'm sorry. I hadn't realised just how important this was to you. Boxwell flew off at dawn, and I could find no-one else who knows anything at all about his staff. In the end I had to give up, because I have only an hour or so left.' His voice tails off as I nod gratefully.

I lose interest in all that goes on about me, while the men go out of their way to give me a wide berth as we pump fuel into the tanks and make the boat ready to receive her new master when he arrives to take command in two days time. I cannot explain my feelings; even to myself, so I speak only when spoken to, and although I know that I am behaving like a stupid OD it makes no difference. Finally, Tod and Froggie can stand it no longer and trap me into an isolated corner of the depotship.

'They have organised a trip to Giza,' says Tod. 'It's for chiefs and POs. We thought you might like to come along to have a look at the pyramids and the Sphinx.'

'Seems a shame to come all the way out here and not see them,' urges Tod.

'Why not?' I ask sardonically. 'Most of us never get past the hooch-houses and knocking shops.'

They exchange glances. 'We didn't think that was your style. We thought your brain was situated somewhere north of your balls,' says Froggy.

'I'm not interested in all that,' I say sullenly. 'I would only be in the way.'

'Look, Ben,' insists Tod. 'Neither of us know a Min from a Mut, or a Seth from a Sobek, but it gets us away from the stink of the boat for a while. It'll do us good to get some dust into our lungs.'

Froggy tries a more blatant approach. 'The truth is that we are sick and tired of watching you moping about the place like an out of work pox-doctor's clerk, and we both know what's eating you.'

'Do you?' I snap, glaring into his face. 'You know sod-all!' His face collapses and I relent a little. 'I know you mean well, but this is something I have to work out for myself.'

'You are not the only one who thought a lot of the skipper. It cut us all up when he died, but a lot of mates are gonna die in this lousy war, and there isn't time to sit about and mope,' he persists.

Suddenly I feel the need to explain. 'If you must know, I feel as though I have been let down.'

'Let down!'

I look away. 'That's right. I backed Martingale in everything he did. Now when I look back I wonder if he didn't overstep the mark. You can't run the navy for individuals. It's all very well to be enterprising, and bend the rules from time to time, but there were times when he seemed more interested in pushing his own ideas than worrying about what he was supposed to be doing. The Andrew's no place for loners; you should know that.'

'Jesus Christ!' exclaims Froggy wearily. 'You've got your brain in low gear, Ben. What about if we had brought it off? Just think of the reception we'd have got if we had brought that battered old U–boat in to harbour!'

He leans forward to talk right into my face. 'You said yourself that war's aint won by people who only obey the rules. Just a few miles east of here is a place called Abuqir Bay, where a whole fleet thought they were safe when they moored up nose-to-tail close in to the beach. They expected Nelson to obey the rules.'

He ticks off each point on his fingers. 'Rule one said that no-one fights a fleet action at night if it can be avoided. Rule two said that you don't sail into a badly charted bay without sounding it out first, and rule three said that no sensible captain would take his ship into the shallows between the anchored ships and shore. So all the French admiral had to do was concentrate his men and armament on the seaward side.'

He stops to draw breath again. 'The snag was that Nelson had been breaking rules since he broke the line at St Vincent, and he wasn't gonna stop now. It was late afternoon, so he could see no point in waiting until morning and allowing the French to bring reinforcements from shore. He decided to sail straight into the bay, even though he left one of his ships stranded high and dry on the corner. As far as he was concerned, she made a bloody good marker for the others to make their turn.

'That Froggy admiral must have had kittens when he saw the British sail right into the gap between his ships and the shore, dropping kedge anchors over their sterns to hold them back while they went down the line on either side, pounding his ships to hell, until only two managed to creep away undamaged.' He leans closer. 'That could have been a bloody disaster. Nelson must have known the risks he was taking with his men and ships, and if anything had gone wrong he would have been condemned for all time; just like you are condemning Martingale now. That is what rule-breakers do, Ben. Thank Christ there are still some about!' He stops, aware that we are both staring at him wide-eyed, and becomes embarrassed as he explains. 'I'm interested in that sort of thing: It's a sort of hobby.'

Tod takes up the cause. 'You're guts-aching about sod-all, Ben. If you want to feel bad about the skipper dying, okay, but don't twist the truth or you will play right into the hands of people like Boxwell. Now,' he goes on more calmly, 'are you comin', or not?'

It is a hot, dusty ride in the back of a three-tonner, but the time passes quickly enough as we ride through the dusty countryside until even the most philistine amongst us falls silent as the pyramids come into view. We have to run the gauntlet of a swarm of hawkers as they try to sell anything from dirty postcards and copies of Fanny Hill, to guided tours and their sisters, but eventually we join the rest of the gawpers and gaze up at the huge pyramids of Cheops and Chephren as they dwarf their half-sized mate, Mycerinus. Even a luke-warm sod like me has to be impressed when I stare up at the peak of the four hundred and fifty foot triangular mound, and try to imagine the sweat that went into putting those massive stones into place.

Everywhere I look there are museums, mausoleums and monuments. Far too much for anyone to take in at one go. So we settle for soaking up the atmosphere and ogling with the crowd at the overpowering structures; allowing our imaginations to do the rest. Somehow we become involved with a group of officers and ex-patriot civil servants who are winding their way towards the Sphinx. I amble along aimlessly, allowing my two chums to do the enthusing at everything we see. I share their wonder to a degree, for I would have to be made of lead not to. But my interest is tempered by the depression still centred in the pit of my stomach.

As we are swallowed up by the shadow of the Sphinx I am aware of an animated guide making a vain attempt to explain it all as he leads from one unfinished sentence to another with hardly a pause for breath. His task is a hopeless one, for the subject is much too big. Yet he is determined to try and condense a month's narrative into a two-hour spiel, and his efforts leaves his audience more confused than ever. We hang on to the fringe, trying to glean some of what he is saying, but I find my mind wandering as I study the faces of his listeners.

My eyes move from face to face until I focus on a small knot of Wren officers keeping to a tight bunch on the far side. I am about to move on when I recognise a familiar profile. For a second or two I try to recall where I've seen it before, and what makes me take an instant dislike to it. The answer hits me with a jolt. It is the haughty bitch from behind the reception desk of that converted hotel at Rothesay.

Without thinking I push my way through the crowd towards her, ignoring the hostile looks and protests as I thrust them aside in my uncouth charge. Vaguely I hear my two mates struggling along in my wake, but my only concern is to get close to that toffee-nosed bitch from the past.

I am causing a great commotion and the guide stops in mid-flow as everyone stares at me. I see her swing her arrogant head in my direction as I plough through the gaping throng. Her face changes from vague curiosity, to annoyance, to half-recognition and concern when she realises that I am heading straight for her.

Everyone is too spellbound to try to stop me. They just peel aside like a bow-wave until I am standing a yard from her, glaring down into her worried eyes. My two oppos catch up, and they are more than a little alarmed. Even to touch an officer can bring a charge of molesting, and I have bruised a few on my way through the crowd. I can see them poised, ready to make a grab at me if I turn violent, for I am sweating and panting as she tries to disguise her anxiety.

'I am looking for Laura Wellington,' I burst out, dragging her name out of the past.

'How dare you intrude like this!' She is rapidly recovering her composure and all the supercilious disdain is coming back. 'If you do not remove yourself this instance I shall have you arrested!'

I feel an urgent tug at my sleeve, but I ignore it. 'Just tell me if you know where I can find Leading Wren Wellington,' I plead between gasps. There are others moving in now. Army as well as Navy officers, ready to pounce if I make a wrong move. 'Easy, Ben!' urges Tod quietly. 'You'll land us all in the cart!'

I glance at his anxious face. 'It's okay; I've not flipped my lid.' I drop my eyes and allow a moment to drain my emotion, then look up at her with a more reasoned approach. 'I'm sorry I came at you like this, Ma'am, but I have been searching for her everywhere, and when I spotted you amongst the crowd I had to speak to you. What else could I do?'

Her face goes hard. 'You can just go away before you land yourself and your colleagues in serious trouble. I am not used to being accosted by lower-deck ratings.' She begins to turn away.

'What do you want with Leading Wren Wellington?'

I turn towards the new voice and find an older, more gentle face peering at me with a touch of sympathy in the eyes. You have to look close to see that she is middle-aged, and although I don't know the rank that goes with the four stripes on her uniform they are enough to engender respect. I search my mind for a plausible reason; knowing full well that I stand no chance if she thinks I am just a matelot trying to locate his girlfriend. I reach into my pocket and pull out the faithful old jeweller's box. 'My captain asked me to deliver this to her, if I could find out where she is, Ma'am.'

She has style this one. An air of authority, and a manner that only comes from someone with a good background and education. She is studying my face intently, as though she is trying to read behind my expression. It is disconcerting, for I suspect that she is seeing more than I want her to see. If we were alone I would not hesitate to blurt out the whole truth, but not now; not in front of this mob.

'What ship are you from?' she asks with a tinge of kindness in her voice.

The crowd is thinning as they lose interest in us; Drifting back towards their guide. The pressure is easing, and Tod's arms slips away. She makes me feel relaxed. '*Tarantula*,' I say calmly.

Her face softens even more. All except the haughty one look at me with new expressions. 'I thought that your captain was killed,' she says gently.

I look her straight in the eyes. 'That's right, Ma'am.' I lift the box and flip open the lid. The sun catches the silver and throws the reflection back unto her cheek. She must take great pains to smooth her make-up, for there is not a blemish to be seen. Now there is a small frown centred on her forehead, and she is looking deep into my eyes. 'How do you come to know Leading Wren Wellington?'

The crowd has moved away now, and the guide has taken up his spiel. We are standing in a small, isolated group, and this is just between her and me. Even the haughty one has mellowed now, though I can feel their eyes on me, and feel a sudden anxiety. 'I – er – met her in Malta,' I stammer. 'We had to take shelter during an air-raid.' I would like to tell this understanding woman all about the way I feel, because I know that she would be on my side, but that is impossible in the circumstances. I just allow my words to fade away.

She reads it all in my face, and I doubt if anyone could keep a secret from her. 'Leave this to me,' she tells the others softly. 'I will follow along later.' She nods at Tod and Froggy too, and like a pair of obedient spaniels they slope off.

She looks up into the wind and vandal-battered features of the Sphinx for inspiration, as though she is seeking help for what she has to tell me, and I have a cold feeling growing inside me when I see the pain in her face.

'Laura is dead,' she says straight out, without taking her eyes from the enigmatic face.

A shadow passes right through me. Somehow I knew she was going to say that, yet the pain bites hard. We are surrounded by noise and vulgarity, yet isolated in our small oasis of stillness. I struggle to loosen a tight throat. 'How?'

She looks at me. Her eyes are dry, but I can see what she is feeling inside as she tries to make her voice matter-of-face. 'It seems that she was taking shelter inside a house with a young Maltese girl when part of the overhanging cliff collapsed. Neither of them could have felt a thing.'

'I see.'

She must have nodded towards Tod and Froggy because they come to stand with me as I stare down at the silver brooch.

'Come on, Ben,' says Tod quietly. 'I think we have had enough of tombs and monuments for a bloody lifetime.'